What Goes Around

WHAT GOES AROUND

A Western Adventure

Tom D. Bryant

Tom D. Bryant

iUniverse, Inc.
New York Lincoln Shanghai

What Goes Around

A Western Adventure

iUniverse books may be ordered through booksellers or by contacting:

iUniverse
2021 Pine Lake Road, Suite 100
Lincoln, NE 68512
www.iuniverse.com
1-800-Authors (1-800-288-4677)

ISBN: 978-0-595-45664-2 (pbk)
ISBN: 978-0-595-69625-3 (cloth)
ISBN: 978-0-595-89966-1 (ebk)

Printed in the United States of America

DEDICATION

This book is dedicated to the early frontier men and women. They braved an unknown wilderness to move and settle further and further west. Their search for a better way of life laid the foundation for the growth of our great nation.

CHAPTER 1

Clinton James was about as down on his luck as a cowboy could get. He thought back on his life. He had been on ten roundups and cattle drives since he was sixteen years old. Now, ten years later, he had little to show for it. Lady, his salt and pepper gray mare, was getting on in years and he knew this would be her last drive.

Clint had been thinking and talking about California and the gold fields as long as he could remember. He knew the gold rush days had long since past, but it had been his father's dream "to go west, all the way to California to see the ocean, maybe even strike it rich," he would say.

His father's dreams died with him somewhere out on the prairie. They were on a trail drive. It had been a dark night. A lightening storm already had the herd spooked when a large Indian war party attacked. They were after as much of the herd as they could get. The Indians had waited until just the right time. They came out of the darkness yelling and firing their rifles and the spooked cattle stampeded.

The Indians had the advantage of numbers and knowledge of the landscape. By morning what was left of the herd was scattered over five miles. Three men lay dead. One was his father.

Old Gus had been on that drive and was chosen to break the news to the then twelve year old Clint James. Clint vowed that someday, when he was old enough, he would finish his father's dream and go to California.

He had come to Texas cattle country with his father as a young child some twenty years ago and had few memories of life before that time. With the railroads coming south as fast as they could lay tracks, his way of life would soon come to an end. It seemed as good a time as any to fulfill that promise he had made so long ago.

He had just finished with a long difficult drive. Drought had forced them far off their usual trails in search of water and grass. They had lost a big part of the herd along the way and his pay was much lighter because of that loss.

Clint, along with ten other drovers, was riding south to wait for the next spring round up. Slim, a tall friendly man who was always talking (when he wasn't singing), turned to Clint and asked, "You've been talking about going to California ain't you?"

Clint nodded, "Yep!"

"Well there's the trail right there," said Slim, pointing at a wide rutted area. The trail continued up the hill and over a well-packed ridge worn bare of grass.

"That's it all right," said old Gus. "California's at the other end of them ruts. It's a lot of miles between here and there, hard ones too.".

Clint stopped and looked up the trail to the top of the ridge for a long minute. The others rode past about twenty feet and turned to watch what Clint would do.

"It would be a long wait until next spring," he thought. The owner had cut the drive far short of the destination and sold out to a much bigger herd for a lot less than they had hoped to get further north.

Clint made up his mind. He had been talking about California and the gold fields long enough. He decided today was the day to quit talking and head out. He turned west on the trail the men had pointed out, promising Lady her own green pasture if they struck it rich.

"So long," said Clint. "Look me up if you ever come to California."

The others turned south mumbling to each other. "He'll be back," he heard Slim say. "Yep," agreed Old Gus.

Three weeks later, riding into the town of Bitter Creek, Clint was broke and wondering if he had made the right decision. When they turned onto the main street Lady's head was low and her hooves were leaving drag marks. The butt of his pistol thumped against the wood of his saddle with every step. The gun had worn a hole through the leather a long time ago. He wore the pistol backwards so he could use a cross draw, but he wore it that way for comfort rather than speed.

"Step high now," he said. Lady raised her head and turned her ears back as if to listen to every word he said. There had been plenty of grazing grass along the way for Lady but Clint had eaten the last of his grub a day or so back. He would have to find work.

"You can get a few days' rest here old girl," he said. Drawing up at the watering trough in front of the livery he loosened the reins so she could drink. His stomach was gnawing at his backbone as he stepped down into the inch thick dust.

He lifted off, his once white, sweat stained hat and slapped the dust off of his worn out cowhide chaps. He stood looking exactly like the cowboy that he was.

"You're a long way off the cattle trails ain't you cowboy?" said a voice behind him, startling him and interrupting his thoughts.

"Yep, reckon so," said Clint. Turning he saw a tall well dressed man in a gray vested suit walking across the boardwalk. The man had just come out a door with a sign over it, *Sutterfield Bank of Bitter Creek.*

Clint walked over to the man, removed his glove and held out his hand to shake. "Clinton James," he said.

"James," the man said, pulling back his hand and taking a half step back. "You're not … ha … one … ha."

"Nope, No, not at all," said Clint. "No kin. I'm not an outlaw. I'm just a cowboy."

"I didn't mean to accuse you. We've got law here in Bitter Creek. We don't allow outlaws or vagrants in town."

"Well I ain't neither," said Clint. He ran his fingers around his waist to the small of his back, as if stretching. He fingered a five-dollar gold piece he kept sewed in his waist band making sure it was still there. He had almost forgotten it himself. It was a trick an old cowboy had taught him a long time ago. "You can't be a vagrant as long as you've got money."

"The name is Sutterfield. Leonard J Sutterfield III," huffed the man. He was all reared back and square shouldered. "I own almost everything in this town. But I aim to change that." He was looking down to the far end of the street at a rundown part of town.

"Well, that's a mouth full all right. Most folks just call me Clint. I could use a few days work if you know of any. I can do most anything as long as its honest work."

"Barely enough work around here for local folks. Can't give handouts to every passerby coming through with gold dust in their eyes," said the banker.

"Well, I reckon that fits me all right," said Clint. "I'll move on then."

"Long ways to the next town, over rough country too," said Sutterfield. "Best I can do is offer you ten dollars for that old horse of yours."

"No thanks," said Clint. "We've been together too long to part company now."

"I have to admire your loyalty to your horse," said Sutterfield, "but I'm a business man. I've made a small fortune over the years supplying the needs of folks going west. Most of those people had big dreams of striking it rich in the gold fields. They seldom do though. It seems like gold is getting mighty scarce"

"So long," said Clint, as he turned Lady west.

"Hold on cowboy." said the banker. "How are you at mending fences?"

"I've done my share," said Clint.

"Well, you look honest enough and you don't look like you're afraid of a day's work either," said Sutterfield. "We had a lightning storm through here a few days back, scared my stock so bad they ran clean through the corral fence. Pay is a dollar a day, all you can eat across the street at the diner, and keep for your horse. Take it or leave it!"

Clint thought for a moment then said, "I'll take it." He tried not to look too anxious as he stepped back down off Lady.

"There's a creek that follows that tree line out back. It's a good place to camp. There's fish and small game too. A man can make out all right back there for a few days. If anyone asks you, tell them I said its OK. The old man out there will show you where everything is."

"Thanks," said Clint.

"You can call me Mr. Sutterfield, everyone around here does," he said over his shoulder as he went back inside his bank.

Clint led Lady toward the livery stable where he was met by an older man who walked with a limp. The man had been busying around always staying within earshot.

"I'll take care of your horse, Mr. James. I overheard your name," said the old timer. "Go on over to the diner and get some grub in your stomach before you fall flat on your face. How long has it been since you've eaten?"

"Is it that obvious? The name's Clint."

"It is to a man that's been there," he said. "Mine's Az, Azaria Cain," he said in a quick, snappy voice. "Go on now, get something to eat. That work will be here when you get back."

"I'm much obliged," said Clint, as he turned reluctantly to go across the street.

"I'll take good care of your horse," said Az. "Go on now."

Clint looked relieved and went, knowing Lady would be taken care of. The sign on the building across the street read, *Sutterfield General Supply Store, Hotel, and Diner.*

Clint walked through the big front door into an open area. Across the room, beside some stairs, was a man behind a picture frame window. The sign over his head said *Hotel.* To the right was a large room full of shelves filled with all kinds of goods.

To the left was a room of tables. Clint went in and found a table beside a window. A large unkempt man sitting behind the counter grunted something as he sat down … *silence for a few minutes!*

"Get out here woman," growled the man behind the counter, his voice rattling the room.

Shortly a small thin woman dressed in a plain straight dress came out of the kitchen. She had cream white skin highlighted by long black hair. She was carrying a glass of water and a cup in one hand and a big heavy coffee pot in the other.

She hurried over to the table. Clint stood up quickly removing his hat, "Morning ma'am," he said.

Startled, she stopped short. She wasn't used to men with manners. Clint was almost a foot taller than she and for a long minute he found himself staring down into the saddest pale blue eyes he had ever seen.

"That coffee sure smells good, ma'am," said Clint, breaking his stare.

She quickly set the water and the cup down. She then poured the cup full of coffee. "What'll it be, Mister?" she asked, her thin lips trying to make a nervous smile.

"Whatever you've got that's already cooked," replied Clint, sitting down.

She turned and hurried back to the kitchen. It was then that Clint noticed two big blue eyes staring over the counter at him. She was on the opposite end from where the man was dozing.

"Could be a doll thought Clint," until the eyes blinked and a small hand came up and pushed some blonde curls to the back of her head.

The woman came out of the kitchen carrying a high rimmed pie pan filled to the top. She also had a plate with a half loaf of bread, a pile of butter, a knife and spoon.

"Venison stew," she said, setting them on the table.

"Thanks," said Clint, trying not to show his hunger. "Sure smells good."

"There's more in back if you want it," she said, looking a little more at ease.

Just as Clint started to take a bite the doll's head popped out from behind the woman. "Are you a real cowboy?" she asked, in her little girl's voice.

"Yep, reckon so." said Clint, "As real as they get anyway."

"What's your name girl?" asked Clint.

"Sarah," she replied.

"Sit down here with me Sarah, and I'll tell you all about it," said Clint. "If you don't mind listening between bites because this cowboy is sure hungry."

"Are you an outlaw cowboy?" asked Sarah, looking at his bandana.

"Nope, sure ain't," said Clint. "Them's fighting words where I come from," he added, with a big grin as he raked his finger across her chin. Sarah hid her face behind her hands and giggled.

"She has never seen a real cowboy," said the woman, turning back toward the kitchen. "Don't let her bother you now."

"She won't," said Clint. "How old are you anyway?" asked Clint.

"Eight," she answered. "I'm small for my age."

"I wasn't much older than that when I went on my first cattle drive," said Clint.

"When you're riding herd behind five or six hundred head of cows, it can get real dusty. This bandana keeps me from getting too choked up."

Later the woman came back and refilled Clint's pan with stew and took Sarah back to the kitchen.

Az came in just as he was sopping up the last bit of the Venison stew with his last crumb of bread. He said something to the man behind the counter then came over to Clint's table. "I told him to put your food on Mr. Sutterfield's tote card."

"Thanks," said Clint, getting up to leave. He looked down at the empty dishes and wondered where he had packed all that grub. He knew he would have to plan better from here on out.

"So you're working for Mr. Sutterfield now are you?" growled the man.

"Yes," said Clint. "For a few days anyway."

A black shiny saddle hanging on the wall caught Clint's eye as he was walking into the stables and he stopped to admire it. It looked completely out of place among the dust and rust of old leather and tools. "That's some saddle," he said.

"Yes," said Az, with a little pride in his voice. "Had a horse under it to match at one time. A man will sell everything he's got if he is hungry enough."

"Well, guess I'd better start earning my keep," said Clint, going out the back.

Clint worked until sundown. Az walked up and handed him a warm cloth with something rolled up inside it. "The girl wanted you to have this," he said. "You can bring the cloth back tomorrow."

"Thanks," said Clint. He led Lady out back to the creek and set up camp. Then he sat down and leaned against a tree. He unwrapped the cloth to find two big slices of buttered bread and two slices of meat and a small sack of coffee.

"Well I'll be doggone," said Clint. "I won't go to bed hungry tonight old girl," he said to Lady. She raised her head, chewing on some grass, and wiggled her ears in agreement.

CHAPTER 2

The next day was much the same until quitting time when Sarah ran up behind Clint and handed him a basket. "Here," she said.

"Thanks," said Clint. "What's your mother's name, Sarah?" he asked.

"Sarah, same as mine," she answered. "Only she's not my real mother. I never knew my real momma and daddy. But Sarah's real nice and she takes good care of me," she said, as she turned and ran away.

When Clint got back to camp, he opened one end of the basket and found more bread and two big juicy steaks that smelled like they needed to be eaten.

He opened the other end and found one of the nicest bone handled straight razors he had ever seen and a half cake of soap. "Well I guess I am in bad need of that," he chuckled, running his hand over three days of stubbles on his face. "I'll put them to good use right after I finish off those steaks," he thought. His razor was about used up and in bad need of replacing.

The next day at noon when Clint went to the diner for lunch, big Sarah and little Sarah were both standing by the door waiting with big smiles on their faces. Little Sarah took his hand and led him toward a table with a cloth on it. "You look real nice all cleaned and scraped," she said. "We've got something special for you since it's your last day," she added. "Sit down and don't look." The rough talking man was nowhere to be seen.

Clint covered his face with his big hat so he couldn't see. Big Sarah disappeared into the kitchen and returned with a big covered plate and set it in the middle of the table.

"OK, you can look now," said little Sarah, removing the cover.

Clint just sat and stared. "They're fish," explained little Sarah. "We caught them yesterday evening just for you."

"Well then you'll both just have to sit right down here and help me eat them," said Clint. It looked like the first time in a while that either of them had done anything that they enjoyed doing.

After they had finished eating, Clint took the razor out of his shirt pocket and handed it back to little Sarah. "I think this is yours," he said.

"I want you to have it," she said. "It belonged to my real daddy."

"Then you ought to hang onto it," said Clint.

"The only thing I know about my daddy is that he was really nice, like you," she said. "So I want you to have it." Big Sarah nodded approval so Clint put it back into his pocket. "Besides, I'm going to marry you when I grow up," she added.

"No," said Clint. "You'll marry someone your own age, a lot better than me." But he couldn't help sitting up a little straighter and holding his chest out a little further.

"Nope," she said. "I've made up my mind, it's you I'm going to marry."

When Clint walked into the stable Az stopped him. "Some advice," he said. "Mr. Sutterfield is a man of his word. I mean he'll do what he says he'll do, but he charges three prices for everything."

"I've noticed that for myself," said Clint.

"Just so you know when you collect your pay," Az. went on. "There's a little trading post about two days ride north of here. It isn't much but you can get what you need and the prices are fair."

"Thanks," said Clint. "I'll keep it in mind."

Clint was just finishing his work when Mr. Sutterfield walked up behind him. "You do good work," he said.

"It'll hold all right," said Clint. "I'll collect my pay now," he added.

The banker reached into his vest pocket and took out two silver dollars. He dropped one into Clint's gloved hand, hanging onto the other one like it was the last dollar in the world. Finally he let go of the second coin, letting it clunk down on the first one. Clint quickly closed his hand around them and shoved them in his pocket.

"How would you like to make a lot more?" asked the banker.

"How much more?" asked Clint.

"Like I said before, we had a lightning storm a while back that scared off all my stock. There are wild mustangs running all over those hills out back, and most of them are mine," said Sutterfield. "I'd pay five dollars a head for up to twenty of them. But no more than twenty."

"I ain't no buster," said Clint.

"Don't need them busted," said Sutterfield. "Just halter train them and lead them back."

"I'll need supplies," said Clint. "Ropes, halters, food. Enough for three, four weeks."

"I'm a business man," said Sutterfield. "How a man treats his animals is a good way to judge his character. I'll stake you for up to forty dollars in supplies." He could see Clint coming around. "I'll even throw in the use of that old pack mule out there. That would still leave you sixty dollars cash. That should go a long ways to getting you to California."

Clint thought for a long minute. "Throw in that black shiny saddle hanging on the wall in there and you've got a deal."

"Done," said the banker.

"Hot dang," said Az, who was always within earshot of everything being said. "I'll get the pack mule ready," he added, as he stomped a little jig in the dust.

"Follow the creek back to the mountains," said Sutterfield. "You'll find a box canyon already fenced. You will have to repair the gate. There is a lean-to cabin inside the fence. Ain't too bad either. It's rough country out there though. Be careful."

"I'll leave at daybreak." said Clint.

It was late in the evening by the time Clint had finished his work and washed up.

The sun was disappearing below the distant horizon as Clint walked toward the diner. He could see one dim light coming from the darkened window as he walked across the street. Most of the town folks had already closed shop and gone home leaving the town shadowy and quiet in the late evening dusk.

Although long past the supper hour he hoped for one more visit with Sarah before leaving. Clint walked across the boardwalk to the big front door and stopped. He knew that Sarah closed as soon as the last customer left at night to get ready for the morning rush. Breakfast came early and she had to be up to cook it.

He turned to leave just as the door popped open. "Come on in," said Sarah. "Coffee's still hot."

Clint turned back toward Sarah looking surprised, “I thought you were closed,” he said, trying not to look too anxious. “But I’m glad you’re not,” he added. He never knew what to say to a lady.

Sarah led the way into the diner. She went to a table where a middle-aged man was just finishing his coffee and standing up to leave. She introduced him as marshal Williams. “Bill Williams,” he said, holding his hand out to shake.

“Clint James,” he said.

“Hear you are going down the valley to hunt mustangs,” said the marshal.

“Yes,” nodded Clint. “At first light in the morning.”

“Rough country,” said the marshal. “You’ll make it OK though if you stay on the horse trails. There are big boulders hiding in that tall grass. Sometimes you don’t see them until you fall over them.”

“Thanks for the advice,” said Clint, as the marshal walked out the door.

Sarah walked to the table with two cups in one hand and her big coffee pot in the other and sat across from Clint.

“You will do well to listen to the marshal,” she said. “He has ridden that country hunting for men that went after those horses. Buried two of them. I wouldn’t want that to happen to you,” she added shyly.

“How did you and little Sarah end up in this dusty old town anyway?” asked Clint. “She said that she didn’t remember her real momma and daddy. That is if its OK to ask? You don’t have to say if you don’t want to.”

“I lived in a small farming community in Illinois. I was seventeen years old and had just finished school to become a teacher when I met Thomas Russell. We fell in love and were married.”

“He was a hard working and ambitious man. Our dream was to have our own farm. He took a full time job in town and I took a teaching job to help out. We saved all we could but a year later it still wasn't enough."

"A man came through town handing out fliers saying *Free Land. Free for the Taking. There's Plenty of Free Land out West for Anyone That Wants It.* He told us that the wagon train was leaving St. Louis in three weeks and that folks were coming from all over. He encouraged us to not be left behind."

"We were young and ambitious. He made it sound like an exciting adventure. It took most of our savings to buy a wagon and team and supplies, but we loaded our few possessions and along with two other wagons set out for St. Louis."

"Things went wrong right from the start. Half the wagons were late getting to the meeting place. We lost valuable time and supplies just sitting and waiting. By the time we were ready to leave there were rumors of an early fall, so our leaders decided it would be best to take a more southern route. That too, would add time to the trip. A few weeks later some of the cattle began to get sick and had to be shot."

Clint just sat and listened to her amazing story without saying a word.

"Later a family got sick with fever and chills, all of them died and the people panicked. They shot their animals and burned their wagon in hopes of keeping it from spreading. Nothing worked. The fever kept spreading. First one got sick, then another until almost half the wagons had sick folks."

"They separated the wagon train. All the wagons with sick folks had to stay at least five hundred feet behind the rest of the train. They gave up trying to burn the wagons or bury the dead and just left them on the trail. One night little Sarah wandered into our camp all by herself. The only thing she had with her was her father's razor and a half-eaten potato. She had lost her whole family. She was just four years old at the time and doesn't remember any of what happened. The only thing she could tell us was her name, Sarah. I hid her in our wagon for a week hoping no one would notice her. I tried to find out who her family was but it was useless. She never showed any signs of the fever, but Tom did. He tried hard to hide it, and did for a few days, but a week later he was down sick."

"The wagon train leader said they had to keep going, that there was a town twenty miles south, we could get help there. They left us there on the bank of Bitter Creek. Three days later I buried Tom on that very spot and I've never gone back. I came here and sold the wagon and horses. I moved into a small room in back of the store and took a job as cook. That was four years ago," she said. "How about you?"

"Not much to tell," replied Clint. "No family. I started working on a cattle ranch when I was twelve years old. Went on my first cattle drive at sixteen and I've been at it ever since until I decided to try my luck in California."

"As far back as my memory goes, I lived on a small dirt farm until my mother died. My father always blamed himself for her death. Time and again he would say the work was just too hard for her. A man can't change what he is, I ain't no farmer."

"Later he packed what food and things we could carry on that one big plow horse and we left. I don't even remember where we were. We moved from ranch to ranch and round-up to cattle drive until we ended up on the Davis ranch. My father was killed in a stampede and buried somewhere out on the prairie. The cowhands took me under their wing and taught me how to ride, rope and shoot."

"Well we both got early mornings," said Clint as he got up to go. "I'll see you before I leave town."

For a brief second Clint thought he might ask her to go with him. It would be nice to see her get away from this place, but he quickly let it go. Out here in the middle of nowhere and broke. He had nothing to offer her and had no right asking. Maybe someday he could, but not with winter coming on. At least here she had a roof over her head and food to eat. She also had little Sarah to think about.

Clint was up early the next morning. He threw the new black saddle on Lady. "How's that feel old girl?" he asked, rubbing the side of her neck. She turned her head to the side as if to inspect the new saddle.

Az led the pack mule out loaded with the old saddle, two long sacks full of rope halters and all the supplies he had asked for.".

Clint mounted up and took the lead rope and said, "see you in a few weeks, Az."

"Luck," said Az.

Chapter 3

Clint followed the creek down the valley most of the day until he drew up in front of the lean-to cabin in the box canyon.

"Looks just the way Sutterfield described it," he said, as he stepped down to stretch. After inspecting the cabin, Clint came out. "Not too bad," he said to Lady as he began to unload his supplies. "It's a lot further down here than it looks from up there."

"You two might as well go on and graze while I set up camp," Clint said, giving them both a pat. Lady headed straight for a patch of clover close to the creek. It was in the shade of a tree.

"It gets dark early down in these canyons," thought Clint. "I'll get settled in and eat, then get some rest. The sooner I catch twenty mustangs the sooner I'll be on my way to California." But his mind kept going back to Sarah.

The next morning Clint walked out of the cabin to see nine mustangs grazing beside Lady. "Well I'll be doggone, way to go girl."

He hurried and emptied one of the sacks of halters and lead ropes and made a temporary rope gate. "That will hold them until I can get some breakfast and repair the gate."

As soon as he had repaired the slide pole gate he called Lady to the cabin and saddled up. "I'm going to have to bust one of them critters, no sense in wearing you out," he told her. Lady nodded and snorted in agreement.

Clint picked a big red stallion, made a loop in one end of his rope and tied the other end to the saddle horn. He hid behind Lady. Then holding onto the loop end of the rope he reached his arm across her neck. Together they walked back out to the mustangs and stopped beside the big red.

When he raised his head, Clint put the loop out around his head, almost spooking him. He stayed still for a minute until the stallion started to graze again. Clint tightened the loop and led Lady back to the cabin with big red in tow.

He pulled the rope tight until the stallion's head was tight against Lady's side. He reached across and put on a halter using the empty sack as a blinder. He then saddled big red using his old saddle. He got up on Lady and slid over onto big red and removed the blinder.

He bucked a little at first. "Easy boy," said Clint. "You've been rode before ain't you? Been awhile though." Clint worked the rest of the day, using the same technique to get halters on the other eight mustangs. The next morning they were all tied out and grazing. Clint saddled the big red, removed the slide pole gate, then went scouting for more wild mustangs.

For the next two weeks Clint got very familiar with that part of the country, and had eight more mustangs to show for his work.

After searching for two days more with no sign of another horse he was about ready to look somewhere else. Then just as he was topping a hill on his return to camp he spotted five mustangs drinking at the creek. He stopped short but they spooked as soon as they saw him and ran for the hills.

One was a big black and could run faster than any horse that Clint had ever seen. He knew he would have to have that stallion before he could ever leave this canyon.

The next morning the mustangs were back. Clint sneaked out as close to the pole gate as he could without being seen and waited, hoping the big black would see his herd and come inside.

The big mustang came within fifteen feet of the gate, sniffing the air, then suddenly turned and ran across the creek and vanished in the tree line over the hill.

The next morning Clint was up early, he moved his string of mustangs over to be in plain sight of the gate and made sure they were tied securely.

He then rode up a ways, crossed the creek and hid in a clump of trees. making sure he was out of sight. He waited all day with no luck and was about to give up the second day when the big black stallion stepped out of the trees and stopped in the middle of the creek to drink.

The big black walked to the gate and stopped half in and half out snorting and sniffing the air. The other four followed.

Clint heeled big red, and letting out a yell, sprang from their hiding place at a full run. Crossing the creek Clint fired two shots from his pistol into the air.

The five mustangs jumped to full speed and ran to the back of the box canyon. His string of mustangs pulled, bucked and whinnied. He stood a good chance of losing them all if they pulled loose, but it was a chance he would have to take. Clint stopped and pulled all three poles in place closing the gate. He stood admiring the big black trying to imagine what it would be like riding so powerful an animal.

He worked with the five horses for a couple of days. As soon as he got halters and lead ropes on them, he broke camp. Tomorrow he would lead them to town, collect his pay and head west.

The next morning Clint wasted no more time than it took to get the old saddle on the big black stallion. He then took the two sacks with about five pounds of rocks in each and threw them across the saddle. "Might as well get you used to carrying some weight," he said.

Clint tied the lead ropes from Lady and the pack mule to his saddle horn. He tied another rope between Lady and the mule. He then tied all the lead ropes to the one in the middle, got on big red and strung them out toward Bitter Creek.

Just as he rounded the last curve in the creek Clint stopped and tied a trace rope between two trees, then tied the big black to it with enough rope to graze and get water. He would leave him here until he returned to make camp, they would stay overnight.

When Clint arrived at the corral Az was holding the gate open for him and closed it when all the mustangs were inside.

Mr. Sutterfield walked out to the corral looking surprised.

"Twenty head, halter trained," said Clint, "and delivered as promised. Reckon I'll collect my pay now."

"Well, come on over to the bank," he said. In his office, Sutterfield counted out the money, "fifty-eight, fifty-nine, sixty. That was our agreement and no more."

"That was our agreement all right," said Clint, walking out the door and back to the corral.

Clint took his saddle off big red and put it on Lady. Then he handed the reins to Az. "This ones for you," he said. "Come and go with me to California."

"I reckon not," said Az. "My traveling days are over. Any way you'll have your hands full just getting yourself and that old horse to California. With the desert to the south and the mountains to the north, it won't be easy. Thanks for asking though. Maybe I'll make it someday. The railroad is coming you know."

"I reckon this is so long then," said Clint, mounting up. He rode across the street to where the two Sarahs were standing, sad faced on the board walk. He said his goodbyes and turned to ride out of town.

"Don't go," he heard little Sarah sob. "Don't go!" Just for an instant he thought he felt Lady hesitate. He urged her on.

Clint couldn't look back. He thought of old Az. He had come here as a young man down on his luck and now, with a bad leg and old age, he might never leave. He hadn't come this far to get stuck in this dusty old town.

When he crossed the creek, he turned south and rode back to where he had tied out the black stallion and made camp. The next morning Clint added five more pounds of rocks to each bag strapped across the saddle on the black, rode back to the road and turned west.

It was almost noon when Clint crested the hill and started down the other side. He turned his head back and watched as the town disappeared below the horizon and out of sight. He couldn't help wonder what would become of Az and the two Sarahs.

CHAPTER 4

When Clint came to the northern trail, he made camp. The next morning he put the saddle on the black and added more weight, but when he mounted up this time he turned north.

"Don't worry girl," he said. "That stallion ain't here to replace you." Lady turned her ears back to listen. "We're headed for the rail head up north. He's our ticket to California."

They had been making slow time the last two days. The third morning when Clint broke camp he loosened the two long leather straps that kept the bags of rocks bound and put them in his saddle bag. He left the two bags of rocks lying beside the trail for anyone coming along to see and ponder.

He saddled the black stallion. "It's time to put you to the test," he said, as he put his old saddle and supplies on Lady. Clint tied the lead rope from the black to the saddle horn on Lady, then climbed in the saddle. At first nothing, then the black stiffened, getting ready to buck.

"Lead out Lady," said Clint. Lady moved forward tightening the lead rope and the black followed as he had every day since they left the canyon.

By midmorning the black was leading and at a much faster pace. Without Clint's weight Lady could travel much faster.

Clint drew up at the top of a small hill on the edge of a clearing. He was about a half quarter across from a log structure situated in a sharp bend of a creek. A big sign over the building's door read, *The Elbo Trading Post.*

Clint headed the black forward slowly.

There was a horse and a mule tied to the hitching rail out front, both saddled. There were two horses in the corral out back.

Clint tied his horses to the rail and stepped inside. A heavyset man with a friendly face stood behind the counter. He smiled, showing a lot of teeth. "Come on in stranger. What can I do for you?"

The man was a little too friendly and a little too glad to see him to suit Clint. He knew he would have to be ready for some kind of trouble.

Two rough looking men were sitting at one of the two tables along the wall on the left side of the room. They had a bottle of whiskey and a deck of playing cards between them. They had stopped talking and were looking hard in Clint's direction. The way they were acting put him even more on guard.

"I need a few supplies," said Clint, walking over to the counter. The two men went back to talking and playing cards.

"What will it be?" the man asked, just as the door banged open. Two more men, just as shabby looking as the other two, walked in.

"These are outlaws for sure," thought Clint.

"You're a long ways off the cattle trails ain't you mister?" asked the man behind the counter. The storekeeper looked as nervous as Clint felt.

"Yep, reckon so," said Clint.

One of the two men who came in was big and rough talking. The other was a smaller, slim, smooth talking man with snake mean eyes.

"If trouble starts, he'll be the one to reckon with," Clint thought as they walked back to the table with the other men. "I need a sack of dried beans, flour, coffee and a box of salt."

While the storekeeper was putting the supplies in a sack, snake eyes stood up and asked, "How much you want for that black you got tied to the rail, cowboy?"

"He ain't for sale," said Clint.

Snake eyes looked meaner than ever, making the man behind the counter even more nervous. He knocked something over crashing it to the floor. Snake eyes sat back down and the men went back to talking.

"How much?" asked Clint. He wished he hadn't put all his pay in his shirt pocket.

"That will be one dollar and seventy-five cents," said the storekeeper. "I've got some fresh salt cured pork if you need it."

All four men turned to watch as Clint reached for his shirt pocket. Instead of reaching in the pocket he rubbed his chin. He remembered the two silver dollars in his pants pocket. He removed his gloves, dug down deep, pulled them out and tossed them over on the counter.

The four men looking disappointed, lost interest, turned back and started talking and playing cards.

"Finish it out in beef jerky," said Clint. He took the sack holding it close to his side. He turned to the right with his back to the men and slipped his pistol from its holster. He walked to the door, hiding the pistol behind the sack. Clint heard chairs sliding across the floor. One chair fell over as the four outlaws stood up.

"Hold it right there," said snake eyes. "We're taking that black horse, mister,"

Clint turned to face the men. He raised his pistol and cocked it at the same time. "Not today you ain't," he said.

"Now hold on cowboy," said snake eyes. "Take the gray and leave. There are four of us. No horse is worth dying for, is it?"

"You can't get us all," said big rough.

"Maybe not," said Clint, looking straight at snake eyes. "But if anyone moves a muscle I'll drop you in your tracks, right where you stand."

"Don't anyone move," said snake eyes. "He's got the drop on us for now. Do as he says."

"Take a sack storekeeper and collect their guns." Motioning to snake eyes he said, "Drop in that little hider you have under your vest too." The storekeeper did as he was told. Snake eyes slowly pulled a small pistol from under his vest and dropped it in the sack. "Now bring that sack over here. You fellows can collect these out at the road. But if anyone sticks his head out the door before I'm out of rifle range, I'll blow it off." He was hoping no one noticed that he didn't have a rifle.

Mounting the black, he rode hard for about an hour until he came to where the creek turned and crossed the road. It was about twenty feet across and two feet deep. Clint rode out to the middle and stopped to let the horses drink, then rode out the other side.

He rode another twenty feet and stopped. He had to know if those men were following him. Turning he rode back into the creek, moving down a few feet where some thick trees were growing on both banks. On the west upstream side he found some good sized boulders and decided this would be a good place to hide and wait.

Clint rode upstream about a hundred feet turning out behind the trees and boulders. He tied the black stallion securely to a tree, then went back and covered his tracks. He hopped up on Lady and rode back to the road. Hiding behind some bushes beside a boulder, he waited.

Lady's gray color blended right in. If he had to face these men, he wanted to be on a familiar horse, and Lady was a well trained cow horse. He could drop the reins if he needed to and she would obey directions by pressing his knee to her side.

Clint didn't have long to wait. Two riders were coming fast. They drew up at the water's edge. It was snake eyes and big rough. "Looks like he came out on the other side," said snake eyes.

"Let him go," said big rough. "We ain't never gonna catch up to him before dark."

"Ain't you tired of riding that mule?" asked snake eyes.

"Yeah, but …" said big rough.

"Come on then," interrupted snake eyes, splashing ahead into the water. When he came out the other side he was not more than ten feet from where Clint was hiding.

Clint relaxed but stayed hidden. He knew it wouldn't be long before they were back, and he was right.

They came back at a gallop and stopped at the creek. "He's took to the water," said snake eyes. "You go up stream, I'll go down. We'll find where he came out."

"He'll be halfway to Cold Springs before we find his trail," said big rough.

"Stop your whining and get going," said snake eyes. "I aim to have that black horse."

Snake eyes rode into the creek and turned downstream. Big rough turned upstream. Clint stayed hidden until Snake Eyes turned a corner and was out of sight before he rode out of his hiding place.

Big rough had stopped right where Clint came out of the water. He had hidden his tracks but big rough was a fair tracker.

Clint stayed in the trees until he was about twenty feet behind the big man. "Put your hands where I can see them." Big rough heard Clint cock his pistol so he knew not to make a wrong move.

Clint took one of the leather strips out of his saddle bag and looped one end around the man's right wrist. "Loosen that gun belt," ordered Clint. "Let it drop." He picked the gun and belt up and laid it across his own saddle, He tied the man's hands to his saddle horn and his mule to a tree.

"Hold it right there," said a voice behind Clint. "Keep them hands where I can see them. I can't miss from here," said snake eyes as he rode right up behind Clint. "Untie him."

Clint heeled Lady's flanks pressing his knee hard against her left side, she answered by springing forward and into a sharp turn.

The surprised horse behind them bucked and reared, sending snake eyes tumbling off backwards. He landed on his back in two feet of water. When he looked up he was staring straight into the barrel of a cocked forty-five with a very angry cowboy behind it.

"Those hands had better come out of that water empty," said Clint, and they did.

Snake eyes started to get up and Clint boxed the side of his head so hard with his gloved hand that he dropped back to his knees. "What did you do that for?"

Clint grabbed hold of his hair and half-dragged him over beside Lady. "I ought to drown you," he said. Taking the other leather strip out of the saddle bag, he tied the man's hands tight. He loosened his gun belt, letting it drop into the water, then took the small pistol from under his vest and put it in his own pocket. "Mount up," Clint ordered. He tied snake eye's hands to his saddle. With both men bound securely, Clint led the horse and mule out to the road facing south.

He tied their reins together. Then he took snake eye's rope and with one end tied his foot to his stirrup, looped it under his horse and tied his other foot to the stirrup. He left about three feet of space and tied big rough's foot to his stirrup, threw it under the mule and tied his other foot to his stirrup. Now the horse, the mule and both men were tied together.

Clint broke a big limb and a small limb off a tree. He tied the big limb between the horse and mule. "So long boys," said Clint. Slapping the small limb across the two animals, he yelled and fired his pistol. They jumped forward, he fired again and they ran south fast.

"A horse may not run very far," thought Clint with a chuckle. "But a spooked mule will run until he drops as long as that limbs slapping his legs. The horse won't have any choice but go along."

"That ought to give me a good head start," he thought, going back to retrieve snake eyes gun belt and the big black.

Clint rode hard until late that night trying to put some distance between himself and those men before he stopped to rest. He didn't light a fire and there was no watering hole, but it would have to do. The next morning he made a small fire and boiled some coffee. He broke camp at daylight promising the horses he would do better the following night.

Five days later he rode into the town of Cold Springs and drew up in front of the Sheriff's office. Clint took the two pistol belts inside. The sheriff looked up as he walked in. "Howdy cowboy, you're a long ways off the trails ain't you?"

"Yes, reckon so," said Clint, as he laid the two gun belts down on his desk. He told his story to the sheriff and described the men.

"I know of them," said the sheriff. "They're no good. I had a run in with them once myself. You should've shot them when you had a chance," he added with a laugh. "It would have saved us all a lot of trouble. Say they were heading south last time you saw them?"

"Yep, fast too. We've got a little thing down south called a Texas runaway" He told the sheriff what he had done to the two men and he laughed, really hard.

"Doggonest thing I ever heard of," said the sheriff. "Wonder where they are now?"

"Depends on where that mule tired out," said Clint. "They may be halfway to Mexico by now."

"Where you a heading Mister?" asked the sheriff. "I didn't get your name."

"North, to the railroad." answered Clint. "James … Clinton James," he answered.

"You're not," the sheriff's eyes narrowed. "No, you wouldn't be. I'm Bill Anderson," he said, holding his hand out to shake.

"I'll need more supplies," said Clint.

"Stones General Store at the edge of town has most everything you'd need," said the sheriff, walking out on the boardwalk beside Clint.

"Thanks. I'll camp at the springs tonight. Be gone first thing in the morning."

"I'll keep an eye out for them outlaws," said the sheriff, "but I don't expect they'll come this far."

Chapter 5

Clint was up early the next morning. He broke camp and filled his canteens before mounting up. He looked back at the quiet little town before turning north.

Nice place, he thought, wondering what it would be like staying in one place. "A man could get used to a town like this," he said to Lady.

A few days later Lady began to act nervous and uneasy, turning her ears from front to back alerting Clint. He hadn't seen anyone along the trail. Except for himself it had been completely deserted, but he could feel the tingling in back of his neck that always warned him of danger.

Someone or something was following or stalking them and had been all day. Clint pulled off the trail and rode up a hill into the tree line. He could see a good distance down the trail in both directions so he stopped, waited and watched. "Could be snake eyes," he thought. Clint watched until about dark and not seeing anything made camp.

The next morning he and Lady were still on edge. At mid-evening he had about decided to back track when he came to a large clearing. There was a creek running across the trail on the other side of the clearing with thick trees and boulders all around. "A good place for an ambush," thought Clint.

He left the trail, circled the clearing. He crossed the creek and rode beside it back to the trail. Seeing nothing, he decided to make camp.

After taking care of the horses and supper, Clint gathered some wood, a lot of it, enough to last most of the night. As it began to get dark, he made his campfire bigger and bigger until it lit a large area. He pitched his bedroll in the shadows at the edge of the light to look like a man sleeping. Then he took his blanket and crawled out onto a boulder in the shadows to keep watch.

Sometime in the night he fell asleep. He awoke the next morning to the sound of birds chirping and the sun breaking through the trees. "Must have been more tired than I thought," Clint said to himself.

Clint stood up to stretch. He thought everything looked normal until he saw buzzards circling about a quarter of a mile to the east and decided he had better check it out.

After breakfast he broke camp, mounted up and turned east to where he had seen the birds. Not knowing what to expect, he decided to ride Lady and lead the black. Lady's ears were directed straightforward and Clint knew that whatever had been stalking them lay somewhere ahead, and not too far either.

Clint pulled up. The carcass of a half-eaten large dog, or wolf, lay between two boulders. "Cat," said Clint. "Big one too, from the looks of them tracks, best not hang around." Just then he heard a rustling sound coming from a stand of bushes to his left. *"Yip, yip, yip,"* he heard.

Clint stepped down drawing his pistol as he walked over to the bushes to investigate. Pushing the leaves aside he found a small pup which he thought was probably not more than a month old.

"Ain't you the lucky one," he said, picking up the little dog. "You look all right, I reckon you'd better come with me though, that cat won't stay gone long."

Just then he heard a loud shrill '*rowl*' from the other side of the boulders, making him and the horses very nervous. He couldn't see the cat but could tell it was getting closer. Clint hurried back to the horses, "It's time to ride," he said as he mounted up and turned back toward the trail at a fast pace.

Clint could hear the cat '*rrowling*' over to his right. Either the cat was moving fast or there were two of them. Clint had invaded their territory and that gave them a big advantage. He was riding uphill on rocky ground through a narrow passage of boulders with overhangs about thirty feet high. Both sides were lined with small trees and thick underbrush.

Suddenly Lady slid to a stop. She was standing perfectly still with her ears pointing forward. The black ran past to the end of his lead rope. He was about to panic. Clint drew him in tight and tied him off. After looking around he decided that there was a lot of clearing back at the trail with plenty of seeing room. He knew the cat wouldn't come out in the open and they would be safe there.

"We're going to have to make a run for it," Clint said aloud. He was about to heel Lady forward when he saw a moving shadow on the ground about twenty feet ahead. "That cat's getting anxious," he thought.

Clint drew his pistol out and eased Lady forward. Staying just under the tree limbs, he waited. The next time the cat raised his head Clint fired. He saw fur flying from the right side of the cat's head and heard a loud screech of pain as the cat ran away. He heeled Lady forward.

Clint held the pup until he got back to the trail. Then he emptied one of the white cloth grocery sacks into his saddle bag with the little pistol he took off snake eyes. He cut a hole just big enough for the pup's head and put him down inside the sack. "You are the lucky one all right," said Clint, poking the pup's head through the hole, "and that's just what I'll call you, Lucky."

Clint tied the sack to his saddle and rode north leaving the cat and the danger behind. Except for a *yip* ever now and then when he needed to stop or was hungry, the terrified little pup was content to sleep most of the time.

CHAPTER 6

He rode until late in the evening before stopping to make camp at the edge of a dry creek bed. There was a good stand of grass for the horses, something he had seen less and less of as they got higher into hill country. He would let them eat their fill.

The little pup was beginning to yap and whine. He was hungry. Clint made a small campfire and poured water from one of his canteens into his pan to boil. Later he put in the last of his beef jerky to make a broth then put in a little flour for thickening. The pup lapped it up like it was the best thing he had ever eaten. "He needs meat, and so do I," thought Clint. "I'll have to take care of that tomorrow."

The next morning when Clint got up there was a light dusting of dew sparkling in the early morning sun creating a warm glow. There was also a chill in the air, the first signs of fall. He broke camp and headed north, higher into the hills. He could see thunder heads boiling up in the sky further north. "Maybe two days ride," he thought.

Traveling uphill was a bit slower and more tiring. It was mid-afternoon when Clint drew up at a small stream about three feet wide. The water was crystal clear and moving downhill fast. He sat as high up in the saddle as he could. He stretched to see up and over a long sloping hill at what looked like a small pond. "Fish," he thought.

Clint rode off the trail about a hundred feet behind some trees and made camp. He tied a rope between two trees over a grassy spot and tied the horses out to graze. He checked all around for clover. Lady had been known to untie her rope to get to a good clover patch.

After tucking the pup in, Clint took his fishing line and started walking up the slope toward the pond. As he walked up over the hill, the little pond turned into a large lake of crispy clear water. Except for a fish jumping here and there it was as smooth and reflective as a mirror.

Clint looked back down the hill for a quick check on the camp. He didn't like leaving the animals unattended, but he would have to if he wanted to catch some of those fish for supper. He took one of the last two pieces of boiled beef jerky and baited his hook. After tying on a piece of driftwood for a float he threw the line as far out into the water as he could. Looping the other end around his wrist he sat back to wait.

It wasn't a very long wait. He was half dozing and deep in thought when something tugged then grabbed his arm. His fishing line was stretched tight. Something was pulling and jerking to get away. It startled Clint out of his thoughts.

He pulled hand over hand until a fish flopped upon the bank. It was a large bass, enough for a meal. "One like you is enough," said Clint, hurrying back over the top of the hill to check on the camp. Seeing everything looked OK he drew his Bowie knife, threw the fish on a flat rock, cleaned it, then started back to camp.

About halfway back Clint saw that Lady had untied her rope and moved closer to camp. Suddenly she reared and stomped the ground with her front feet.

Clint was moving faster now. About a hundred feet away he saw what Lady was stomping at. A large black snake was circling the camp. "He's after the pup," thought Clint. Ever time the snake would make a dash for the little pup he was met by two very fast and deadly hooves.

Clint dropped the fish and hurried around behind Lady so he wouldn't distract her attention away from the snake, if he did she would surely be bitten. When Clint walked up beside Lady, he saw a bloody and badly beaten snake that refused to give up. It had crawled out away, stopped and turned around to come back. When he raised his head Clint fired one shot ending the struggle.

Lady walked over to the saddle and nudged it up with her nose. Out rolled the pup, unaware of the danger he had been in. Clint checked Lady over good for bites before going back for his fish and making a campfire to cook it on. As soon as it was done, he pinched off a piece on his finger and stuck it in front of the hungry little pup. He eagerly bit down on the fish and the finger. "Ouch," said Clint, jerking his finger back. "Them teeth sure are sharp." They ate their fill then settled in for the night.

The next morning as Clint was breaking camp he could hear thunder in the distance. The storm was getting closer. He had better find shelter, maybe for a day or two.

Clint rode until early afternoon making good time. It was a lonely trail this time of the year. Being so close to winter most everyone had already made it up north or would wait until next spring.

It had started to sprinkle rain when Clint stopped at the edge of a dry wash creek bed which was about thirty feet wide. It was covered with sand, gravel, rocks and boulders. There were four or five small streams of water a few inches deep. The streams were fed by a waterfall splashing over a cliff, overfilling a pool, then running down the hill following the tree line.

Across the wash and up the hill about twenty feet was an overhang about fifteen feet wide. It was about seven feet high then gradually wedged down to the ground. It wasn't much but it was high and dry. It would have to do.

Clint unloaded his gear under the overhang. He took the horses across the trail and tied them out in a field of mostly weeds, but there was some grass down close to the ground.

When Clint looked up, he saw a herd of deer grazing just past the tree line about a half-quarter mile downstream. "Meat," he thought. "I'll get one of them critters if I have time before the storm hits."

Soon he was dragging in large limbs and any other dead wood he could find. Stacking it from the ground to the top of the overhang on the east side. He would need these for both a wind break and for firewood until the storm had passed.

The overhang wasn't big enough for the horses to get completely under so he covered the other end and half the front with branches. He saw some small willows growing along the bank and cut some of those to pile on the branches. Then covered the whole structure with dry leaves.

Clint brought the horses back to camp and backed them in under the makeshift lean-to. "It ain't much but it'll keep you from getting too wet."

The lightning and thunder were getting closer and faster. It began to rain as Clint started down the tree line to where he had seen the deer grazing. The wind had picked up by the time Clint arrived at the grassy field.

All the noise should cover up any sounds he made as he got closer to the deer. The deer were coming toward the trees for shelter. Clint picked a small buck. He hid and watched until the deer was within five feet and fired two shots. The buck was his. He took what he wanted, enough for about three or four days, and left the rest for the scavengers.

Soon he was back in the dry with a big fire blazing and venison cooking. Lucky was sitting next to him, not much bigger than his tin cup, excitedly wagging his tail in anticipation. "It ain't beef," he told the pup, "but it is meat." They ate their fill and settled in for the night.

Sometime in the night Lady began acting up, alerting Clint, not that he could sleep. "Something's out there," he thought. "What is it girl?" he asked.

Clint walked out to the edge of the overhang, staying just out of the down pouring rain. The lightning and thunder were continuous. He squatted down beside a small boulder and scanned the tree line out front.

"If anyone's out there you best show yourself," yelled Clint at the top of his voice. "Come on into the light. Keep your hands where I can see them."

Clint backed over to his saddle bags and took out the small pistol. "Ain't very powerful," he thought, as he crawled back to the boulder "but it is loud." "You've got five seconds before I start shooting" he yelled.

He fired four fast shots out into the night, keeping his forty-five fully loaded, then two more. Suddenly there was a loud shrill growl and the sound of limbs breaking. He heard a thump like something falling from a tree and saw what looked like a large black hairy animal standing facing him in the lightning flashes. Whatever it was turned and ran up the wash. "Too big to be a bear," he thought. "It could be the lightning playing tricks on my eyes though. No, it had to be a bear."

Clint settled back against a rock next to the fire. With his pistol in his hand he covered up with his blanket to keep watch for the night. "I can sleep tomorrow," he thought. Lucky hopped up on his lap and curled up for the night. "Looks like this rain has settled in for a while."

Clint slipped off to sleep just as the morning sky was showing its first light. He awoke to a tugging on his blanket. It was Lucky. He had a corner of blanket in his mouth, growling and shaking his head from side to side as if to say, "Wake up, it's morning and I'm hungry."

"Looks like you're recovered all right," said Clint, taking up the pup to pat. He added some wood to the fire, then put some venison on one of the flat rocks to warm. He put some coffee on to boil.

Later he put on his poncho and took his pan to get water for the horses because the wash had turned into a thirty-foot wide creek of rushing water. The rain had slowed some so Clint pulled some grass to go with the water. "That'll have to do for now," he said to Lady. With a tired sigh he laid down for some much needed sleep.

It was late evening by the time the rain had passed and Clint took the horses out to graze. "Eat your fill. We'll leave at daybreak in the morning."

Clint walked back to the tree line across the wash from his camp. Whatever he had seen had fallen or jumped from about thirty feet up. It broke four or five limbs on the way down and was still able to get up and run. It could've been a bear but he had heard of big hairy manlike creatures roaming these hills and he just may have seen one.

Chapter 7

Clint broke camp the next morning at daybreak and headed north.

It was late evening. They had been traveling uphill all day and it was beginning to wear on the horses. Clint spotted smoke coming from the tree tops over the next rise. He drew up to listen. They had crossed a lot of washes across the trail and saw plenty of damaged trees all left by the storm.

Clint decided to investigate the smoke. “Maybe a camp, even a friendly face,” he thought. When he reached the top of the rise Clint could see another wide wash crossing the trail and a burning tree. “Lightning got it most likely,” he thought. When he drew up at the wash he scanned all around the tree line. “Good place to camp,” he said aloud.

The days were still plenty warm but the nights were beginning to have quite a chill. That burning tree would take some of that chill off, he thought, as he tossed some of the burned off limbs back into the fire.

Clint made camp a little higher up in a grassy area with trees and boulders on the side of a steep hill. Here it would be hard for anyone to slip up behind him.

Lady was still acting up, turning her ears from front to back. Clint wasn't sure that whoever or whatever was following them wasn't still out there. It raised the hair on the back of his neck every time he looked back down the trail, and that made him very uncomfortable.

After supper he brought the horses closer to camp. He was a light sleeper and he hoped that Lady would alert him of any danger. "Get some rest old girl," said Clint. "It looks like we'll be going downhill for the next couple of days starting tomorrow."

Clint rolled up in his blanket with his head on his saddle and his pistol in his hand. Lucky curled up in his usual place under the saddle for a night's rest.

The next morning Clint was startled awake by a growling sound. He rolled over to find himself staring face to face with a crouched, snarling wolf not more than three feet away.

"Hold," said a voice in the background. "Don't move a muscle or that wolf will have you for breakfast, pilgrim."

Clint laid as still as he could. He was still holding his pistol under the blanket and decided to cock it the next time the man spoke.

"Not very smart letting someone ride right up in your camp like this pilgrim," said the man.

Clint had quietly cocked his pistol, the wolf growled even more and began to inch closer. "Hold wolf," he yelled. "You'd better mind me or I'll shoot you myself."

Clint's eyes glanced to the right where Lady and the black were tied. They looked OK but he wondered why Lady hadn't alerted him.

"That's right pilgrim, I aim to take your horses." said the man. "This one is all used up."

The light was coming fast now as the sun was coming up. He was a huge bearded mountain man, 250, maybe 300 pounds, at least six feet six inches tall and dressed in buckskins from head to foot.

He was sitting on an old horse that was too small for him, not much more than skin and bones. That told Clint that he was a cruel and heartless man. The horse kept shifting her weight from one leg to the other under her heavy load.

The man sat slumped in the saddle with his rifle in one hand and his reins in the other. The rifle was laying across his legs pointing toward Clint.

Clint's mind was racing for a way out of this mess. Lucky charged out from under the saddle barking and growling. Just for an instant the wolf's eyes moved. Startled he jumped back. Clint raised his pistol from under the blanket and fired when the wolf was no more than two feet away. He hit the wolf dead center of his chest knocking him backwards and startling the mountain man's horse.

Clint's second shot found its mark, hitting the man's shoulder. The old horse tried to rear, but stumbled. The mountain man thumbed back the hammer of his rifle and fired straight down into the ground.

The old horse reared all the way up and over. As the big man grabbed for the saddle horn something snapped sending the man, saddle and all, flying in one direction and his rifle in another. The old horse kicked loose from the saddle and ran west up a long grade into the tree line and out of sight.

Clint heard the air go out of the man. He had landed on some roots spiraling from under a tree and was knocked out cold.

He took the rope from the man's saddle and tied his hands behind his back. He looped the rope up around his neck, back to his hands again, then down to tie his feet. When Clint rolled the man over, his eyes popped open. "All hogtied and ready for branding," said Clint.

"What are you aiming to do?" asked the man, showing some fear in his eyes.

"Don't know." replied Clint. "Ain't decided."

He retrieved the man's rifle and laid it next to his own saddle and checked on the pup, "Guess you earned your place today little fellow," said Clint.

Lady had untied her rope and was sniffing around on the little pup. The pup snorted. He was getting used to being fussed over and didn't seem to mind.

Clint took the man's knife and cut the seams of his jersey and dressed his wound.

"How long you been following me anyway?' he asked.

"Been hearing you for four maybe five days," said the man. "Been smelling you for two."

Clint piled his bedroll and a canteen in front of him.

"You can't leave me out here afoot like this," said the man.

"Yes I can," replied Clint. "I'll leave you any way I want to."

"That horse of mine won't stop until she gets to Beaver Creek," he said.

"Well if you ever catch up with her you can thank her for saving your life," Clint said.

"That old nag," said the man.

"Yes," said Clint, "I wasn't aiming at your shoulder mister. If she hadn't reared when she did, you'd be laying out there with that wolf. And if you ever get another horse I'd suggest you take better care of it."

Clint broke camp and was ready to leave. He went back to the man. "There's a town four or five days south of here or you can go back the way you came, makes no difference to me," said Clint. "If you walk day and night you might even make it before you bleed to death," he added as he untied the man's hands.

"What about my rifle?" asked the man. "You can't leave me out here without a gun. Every predator in these hills is on the prowl, fattening up for winter. I won't have a chance," he added, as he untied his own feet.

"Better chance than you gave your horse," Clint said, standing back about ten feet. "Your knife's rolled up in your bedroll, it'll have to do. Now start walking."

Clint waited until the man was about a hundred feet across the wash and yelled, "Hey mountain man, see that dead limb off to your right?"

The man looked just as Clint fired the rifle and the limb exploded.

"If I see you on the trail following me, I'll finish what I started," Clint yelled.

He watched until the man was out of sight then turned north at a fast pace.

Lady's ears were directed straightforward. The uneasy feeling was gone.

CHAPTER 8

It was two weeks later when Clint rode into the town of Orchard, one of many that had sprung up along the railroad going west.

Clint followed the tracks past about a half-acre or more of holding pens, toward the station house. He could see an older man standing on the loading dock which was built about five feet above the ground. He was a short thin man, wearing a black and white striped shirt with arm bands and a leather bib apron that said he was probably the station master. His long bill visor cap with a black band stretching around his head allowed his gray hair to blow in the wind and the bright sun to create a halo look.

Clint drew up at the hitching rail and sat looking puzzled at the little man. He was standing like a statue looking off in the distance and holding his watch up by the chain at eye level. He squinted as if trying to see something away off that just wasn't there. He took a quick glance at his watch and then at Clint. He turned, dropping his arm.

"Telegraph line's down," he said. "Sent a work crew out, should've been back by now. You lost?" he asked.

"Nope," said Clint, stepping down.

"Bet you're thirsty though," said the man, pointing at a pump at the back of the platform and walking toward it.

Clint walked around the platform to the back where a big watering trough came through the corral fence to right under the pump. He tied the horses to the fence to drink. The little man started pumping the handle up and down until a small stream of water came out.

Clint laid his big hat up on the platform, removed his bandana and stuck his head under the stream of water, then took a long drink. "Thanks," he said, drying his face with the bandana.

"Elbert Weatherspoon," he said, "just call me Elb. I'm station manager, telegraph operator and everything else around here."

"Clinton James," he said, waiting for the usual response that didn't come. "You can call me Clint."

"Yip, Yip!"

"What's that?" ask Elb.

"Just a little fellow I found out on the trail," said Clint. Cupping his hands he filled them with water and held it under the pup's nose to drink. "He needs a home though," he added.

"You heading west?" asked Elb, watching the pup drink.

"I am." answered Clint. "How far can that train take me?"

"Ain't you heard?" said Elb, "It's all the way to California now."

"You looking for gold?" asked Elb.

Clint nodded.

"Not many strikes it big you know," said Elb. "Reckon you'll want to sell them horses. I'd be interested in the gray, if you ain't asking too much."

"She'll stay with me," said Clint.

"All the way to California?" questioned Elb. "Might be a problem. Costly too."

"One way or the other," said Clint. "I was counting on getting a good price for the black though."

"Go back the way you came, turn left at the end of the corral and go until you come to the stock office," said Elb. "Ask for Mr. Clark. He'll give you as good a price as any. Price charts posted on the wall inside the station house," said Elb, going back to the other side of the platform to look down the track. "You can leave the pup with me," he added.

Clint took his old saddle up the steps and laid it against the wall next to the door and went inside to check the price charts.

When Clint came out he put his new saddle on Lady and followed the directions to the stock office. A man standing on the porch with a big grin said, "Howdy," as Clint drew up at the hitching rail.

"Howdy," said Clint, "I'm looking for Mr. Clark".

"That would be me," said the man.

"Elb over at the train station said you'd offer a fair price for the black."

The man walked down the steps and around the stallion, looking him over good. "Fine looking horse," he said. "Thirty dollars, best I can do."

"He's worth twice that," said Clint.

"Down south maybe," said Clark. "We got the same problems up here with horses as you got down south with beef, too many!"

Throw in the gray and that fancy saddle and I'll up it to fifty dollars," said Clark.

Clint turned and mounted up to leave, he never was one to haggle price and he wasn't about to start now.

"Now hold on cowboy," said Mr. Clark. "I'll make it forty dollars for the black but that's my best offer."

Clint thought for a minute. "Deal," he said, getting back down.

"I'll need a bill of sale," said Clark, leading the way into the office. "Can't believe I raised my own bid," he said, shaking his head.

When Clint signed the bill of sale, *Clinton James*, the man stared long and hard at it, then looked at Clint. "Nope, no kin," chuckled Clint.

"Guess you're used to that reaction," said Mr. Clark.

"Yep," said Clint. "It seems to follow me around."

The two men walked outside and shook hands. "Nice doing business with you," said Clark.

"Same here," said Clint, as he mounted up and rode away.

When Clint returned to the train station Elb was waiting on the steps looking excited.

"You still determined to take that horse to California?" asked Elb.

"Yes, I am," said Clint. "I may have to find a job first though."

"I might be able to arrange it." said Elb. "She'll be free freight, if you're interested."

"I am," said Clint.

"Might even pay a little," said Elb.

"Now I'm real interested," said Clint. "Keep talking."

"You see them two thoroughbred racing horses over there?" asked Elb.

"I see them." said Clint.

"Well they belong to a rich Englishman and his wife," said Elb. "They had that long car over there converted special back east just to ship them across country in." Elb continued. "It's got a small room up front with a fold down sleeping bunk. The car got here about two weeks ago and the caretaker was missing. No one knows what happened to him."

"How's all that going to help me?" asked Clint.

"They need someone to ride in the car with the horses," said Elb. "There's three stalls in back of that car, I've been inside it, seen them myself."

"It'll be a free ride for you and your horse all the way to Sacramento, California," said Elb. "If they agree, that is."

"How do I get this job?" asked Clint.

"Be back here after lunch," said Elb. "I'll introduce you to to the owner."

"Where's a good place to eat?" asked Clint.

"Straight across from where you was awhile ago," said Elb.

Just as Clint arrived at the diner, Mr. Clark was coming out. "You can tie your horse over by the feed trough if you want," he said. "You can keep an eye on her out that window."

"I'd be obliged," said Clint. "She will too."

"Think nothing of it," said Clark, walking across the wide well-packed and rutted street.

Clint led Lady through a wide gate which had been swung back and tied open. The gate led into a large empty somewhat oval shaped corral that showed signs of a lot of use. One end was a long hall with about twenty stalls, each with its own door that opened on the corral side.

He noticed two teenaged boys leaning against the wall holding scoop shovels. They looked surprised when he walked through the gate. A strong smell of tobacco smoke was coming from their direction. Clint tied Lady's lead rope half way between the watering trough and the feed trough. When he turned around the boys had disappeared but the smell of smoke still lingered in the air.

He crossed the street and pushed through a big door into a smoke filled Diner. He made his way across the crowded room to the one empty table with a view across the street. He ordered today's special since it was the only thing on the menu!. Surrounded by strangers he sat listening to the loud talk and laughter of the buyers, sellers and traders trying to make the best deals possible before the last big sale of the year.

As he waited for his food, he thought back across the twists and turns of the long trail he had just traveled. He remembered all the good times and realized he missed the friends he had left back on the cattle trails, but he was looking forward to the future and all the new friends he would have.

When he finished his meal and looked up he saw Lady coming through the gate, her head low. She was dragging her lead rope to one side being careful not to step on it. Clint hurried across the street to meet her, glad to be back outside in the fresh air. He knew that if Lady was ever to make it to California it would have to be on the train. He was more determined than ever to have the job that Elb had told him about. He started toward the train.

He went only a short distance before he knew why Lady had left the food and water. A loud gonging sound turned him around fast. Men were running from every direction toward the corral. He could see black and white smoke boiling from under the roof of the barn.

Clint thought of the two boys as he hurried back to help. "It's out," Mr. Clark announced, coming out of the barn. "I'm obliged to all of you for your help."

As the crowd thinned going back to their business, Clint turned to Clark. "The two boys with scoop shovels," he said as he imitated smoking a cigarette. Clark nodded, "Thanks."

Clint was back at the station at one o'clock sharp. He could see Elb out front talking to a man and woman.

"Here's the young fellow now," Clint heard him say as he rode up.

Clint climbed out of the saddle and held out his hand to shake, "Clinton James," he said.

The woman drew her breath and covered her mouth with a handkerchief that she had tied to her wrist somewhere and moved closer to her husband.

"Don't worry ma'am," said Clint, removing his hat. "I'm just a cowboy."

"These are the Greens. All the way from England," said Elb.

"Howdy ma'am, Mr. Green," said Clint, shaking the man's outstretched hand.

"How much do you know about thoroughbred horses?" asked Mr. Green in his English accent. "They're high strung animals you know."

"Not a thing," said Clint. "But I know all there is to know about mustangs. They're about as high strung as it gets."

"Well at least your honest. Mr. Weatherspoon has told us your circumstance."

"I think you can do the job," he said. "If you want it."

"I'll take it," said Clint. "Elb already said what you wanted."

"You can move into the car right now if you want. Get it ready, get familiar with the horses and be ready to move out at seven a.m. the day after tomorrow," said Mr. Green. "There's a special mix of feed in the car for them and more will be added as you go along," he added.

"Once you're on the way you'll have to walk them back and forth in the car at least twice a day so they don't get too stiff." Mr. Green went on, "All your meals will be brought to you in the car. Is that satisfactory?"

"Yep, reckon so," said Clint.

"Mrs. Green and I will take the next train, in about three hours," he said. "We'll meet you at the station in Sacramento when you arrive.

You deliver both horses in good condition and I'll pay you four hundred dollars."

"You've got a deal," said Clint.

"Then we'll see you there," said Mr. Green.

Clint got settled in the little room at the front of the box car and walked outside. "Come on girl," he said to Lady. "We might as well get to know them two critters. We're going to be living in close quarters with them for the next week or two."

Clint led Lady out to the corral where the two big race horses stood watching every move he made. He stepped between the fence rails and stood facing the two horses. They stomped, snorted and moved around nervously.

"Well they are high strung all right," Clint said to Lady. "But I reckon I can handle them as soon as they're used to us being around." He leaned back against the rail fence and watched.

The next evening Elb walked up to the fence. "Better be getting aboard," he said. "They'll be hooking you up before dark.

Elb watched as Clint led the three horses into their stalls. "You'll pull out at seven-o-five in the morning," he said.

"Thanks for all you've done," said Clint. "I'm much obliged."

"No thanks needed," said Elb. "Just strike it big when you get out west."

"I'll do my best," said Clint. "Look me up if you ever get out there. Take care of Lucky."

The old man nodded and smiled as he turned and walked away into the late evening sunlight.

The first day on the rails went well. An old cook came through the door from the adjoining car carrying a big plate of food and a bucket of water with a dipper in it. Clint was startled and jumped to his feet.

"Might as well relax," said the old cook. "You've got a long ride ahead of you. Name's Joe. I'll be in twice a day."

"Clinton James is mine. What do you know about the gold mines out west?"

"There are lots of tent towns full of panhandlers and prospectors," he answered. "But there's not many gold mines left." Each day Joe would spend some time telling Clint about a different mine that he knew of. Soon they were swapping stories, Joe of his life on the rails and Clint would tell of his out on the cattle trails.

Joe would come back at night after hours. He would bring his coffee pot and tell Clint of another gold mine that he had heard about while waiting tables in the dining car.

Chapter 9

After a while the days turned into a week. Clint lost count of how many before the train at long last arrived at its destination.

"End of the line," someone yelled, as old Joe came through the door to say goodbye.

The big door slid open and a very tired, dirty and weary Clinton James stepped out onto the loading dock. He took a big deep breath, filling his lungs with fresh clean air. After being cooped up with three horses so long, it felt good. "I need a bath, shave and a week's rest," he thought. He could almost smell a thick juicy steak cooking.

Not seeing the Greens anywhere, Clint led the three horses, one at a time, out and down the ramp. As he tied them to the hitching rail he thought he heard someone calling.

"Here, over here. We're coming." Clint heard a familiar English voice say. He turned to see the Greens coming across the street.

"You're here my good man," said Mr. Green. "You're here all right."

"That I am," said Clint. "With two thoroughbred horses delivered, and in good condition. Can't say the same for myself though. I'm in bad need of a bath."

"Let's cross the street to the bank and get you paid," said Mr. Green. "There's a wonderful hotel at the end of the street. It has all the conveniences. I'm sure it will meet all your needs."

Mr. Green turned and talked to the older gray haired man who had walked up behind them. "Yes sir," said the older man, then he took the two big horses and led them off down the street.

They turned and walked across the street to the bank where Clint collected his pay. "Four hundred dollars," he thought. "Enough for a new start."

When they walked out the door onto the boardwalk, Mr. Green surprised Clint.

"Mr. James, my wife Edie and myself talked it over," he said, trying to choose just the right words. "Well, we would like for you to come to work for us. We have a small horse ranch on the coast," he said. "We could use someone with your knowledge of horses and it would pay well."

"That's mighty tempting. You're a generous man, Mr. Green. I thank you for the offer, but I reckon I'll finish what I started. I'll need directions to a stable."

"Across the street from the hotel," he said. "Waldo. My name, I mean, it's Waldo Green. Our ranch is due west of here, all the way to the coast. The job will be there waiting if you ever change your mind." They said their goodbyes and went their separate ways.

Clint led Lady around the corner and stopped at the entrance to the stables where a tall young man with long blonde hair hanging down into his eyes was cleaning. Clint stared across the street at the big multi-story hotel.

"Wow," he said, as the young man walked up beside him. "That is some fancy hotel."

"Yes sir, it sure is," said the young man. "Mostly rich folk stay there."

"Is there another place in town?" asked Clint.

"Yes sir," said the young man, looking all around as if to make sure no one was around to hear. "Just follow the tracks north to the old town square. The old Stockman's Hotel is real nice. They have their own stables and blacksmith shop. They'll take good care of your horse there too."

Just as Clint started to mount up, a slick looking man came out of a door marked *OFFICE*. "You need to get on out back and take care of the animals. *NOW BOY*!" he yelled at the young man, as he walked towards Clint. "Are you looking to stable your horse mister?"

"No thanks," said Clint. "Just passing, taking in the sights."

"Information center is the other side of the train station," the man grumbled, as he turned back toward the office.

Clint turned on North street to the town square and drew up in front of the stable. "This is more to my liking," he said to Lady, as an old stockman came out to meet them.

Clint stepped down as the man took hold of her reins, "Easy girl," he said as he looked her over good. "You two have been a long ways," he said.

"That we have," said Clint. "We need three or four days rest."

"You've come to the right place," said the old man. "Name's Carver, Ace Carver. I run the place. Don't see many horses like her around here," said Ace. "I'll take care of her myself."

"Thanks. Clinton James is mine," he said. "She'll need a lot of rest."

He left Lady in the good hands of the old stockman and checked into the hotel.

After buying new clothes and cleaning up he sent his old clothes out to a Chinese laundry to be washed and went to bed for a good night's sleep.

The next day Clint checked on Lady then went out to see the town. Everywhere he went was crowded full of people that were in a hurry to get somewhere else, so he gave up and went back to the hotel. At the hotel he learned as much about prospecting for gold as he could.

Three days later Clint checked out of the hotel. He had checked on Lady every day. They were both rested and anxious to get out into the open.

"Leaving all ready?" asked Ace.

"Yes," said Clint. "Town is too crowded."

"Well it is that," said Ace, "but a man gets used to it."

Clint had learned from Ace that the Lost Ravine Gold Mine was one of the richest strikes around. He decided that was where he would try his luck. He left his old saddle with Ace who said he would put it on the next supply wagon heading north. "After sitting in it for ten years its kinda hard to just leave it behind," said Clint. "It's kinda like home."

"I reckon so. Just stay on the supply road, due north all the way to Pineville," said Ace as he checked Lady over good. "You'll be OK. The railroad is half way there by now, I reckon."

"Thanks," said Clint.

The old man nodded. "Just ask for Smithy at the blacksmith shop in Pineville," he said, handing Clint a paper. "Give this to him and he'll give you directions from there." Clint turned and rode north.

It was sometime later that Clint rode into Pineville and found Smithy hammering away at the blacksmith shop. He could have been Ace's brother, but Clint didn't ask.

Clint climbed out of the saddle and walked over to the man. "You Smithy?" he asked.

"Who's asking?" said the old man.

"Clinton James," he answered, taking the paper out of his saddle bag and handing it to him.

After reading the paper, he looked Clint over. "Friend of Ace's are you?" he asked.

Clint nodded.

"How is the old coot anyways?" asked Smithy.

"He seemed to be faring well," said Clint, watching the old man as he carefully checked Lady.

"Nice horse," he said, checking the exact same place that Ace had, paying close attention to her legs. "She's getting old though."

"We've been together a long time," Clint said.

"I see she favors oats," said Smithy. "She can rest here while you get supplies across the street. Good place to stay the night and to eat, too."

The next morning when Clint returned, Smithy led Lady out to meet him. "To get to the Lost Ravine," he said, "just follow the supply road west to the river. They are building a trestle straight across at that point because the railroad is coming. Turn north for about ten miles until you come to a low water crossing. From there go west across the river and follow the road another ten miles or so to where the two rivers fork. The Lost Ravine sets right in the fork."

"Thanks," said Clint. "I'll find it."

"I'll send your saddle on when it gets here," said Smithy. "Take good care of the Lady now."

Clint nodded. "That old stockman sure got a lot on that paper," he thought as he turned west.

When Clint arrived at the low water crossing he stopped. It was a long way across but it didn't look deep. "We'll camp on the other side," he said to Lady as she splashed across to the other side. Clint made camp for the night beside the river in a camp site that looked like it had been well used over the years.

When he bedded down for the night, for the first time in awhile, he felt comfortable with where he was.

CHAPTER 10

The morning sun was high as Clint was finishing his coffee and breaking camp. He had slept like a log to the sound of the running water and was now deep in thoughts of striking it big in the gold fields.

Suddenly Lady's head went up interrupting his thoughts and alerting him that someone was coming. She sniffed the air and her ears turned toward the other side of the river.

Clint stood and walked toward the sounds of clinking and crunching he could hear over the sound of the river. Just as he walked out of the trees, he saw a six-mule team pulling a large supply wagon charging into the water on the other side and coming his way.

A man was standing in the wagon urging the mules on. "Hee-yaw," he yelled. "Pull, pull, hee-yaw," his voice came ringing across the early morning water, as he flicked the reins with a loud "snap, snap!"

Clint watched them all the way across the river. "Hee-yaw, pull, pull, pull," the man shouted. "Snap, snap" went the reins. Their muscles rippled as the mules pulled their heavy load out of the water. The wagon was stacked high and was covered with a canvas that had been tied down tight all the way around.

"Whoa, whoa," he said pulling back on the reins and stopping right in front of Clint. He was surprised at the size of the mules and the wagon. Pushing his hat to the back of his head, he looked up and nodded. "Morning," he said.

"And a cheery morning right back at you," said the man in an Irish accent. A friendly smile suddenly appeared from beneath his sandy red beard. He had hair to match with the big arms and chest of a man that was used to hard work.

"You'd be Clinton James, I'm guessing." said the man. "And that's Lady over there."

"You'd be right," said Clint, looking puzzled. "If you're guessing."

"Smithy said I might be passing by you out here and to keep an eye out for you."

"Dody McAllister," he said. "Throw your gear up and tie your horse on the back. Looks like she could use the rest and I could sure use the company."

Clint did as he said and climbed up into the spring board seat next to the big man.

"Hee-yaw, pull, pull, pull," he yelled, as he snapped the thick leather reins. "Hee-yaw."

"Everyone calls me Irish, easy to remember," he said.

"Clint. Same here."

"Ever drive a six-mule team?" asked Irish, handing Clint the reins.

"Nope," said Clint.

"Time you did," said Irish. He showed Clint how to hold the reins between his fingers to keep them from getting tangled.

"Now bring them up high and back down fast and up again. Make them snap."

Clint did but all he heard was "pop, pop."

"That's OK," said Irish. "You'll get the hang of it. You have to talk to them or they'll slow to a stop," he said. "Pull, pull, pull, like that."

Clint tried to snap the reins a few more times but all it did was irritate the mules.

"Better let me take it now," said Irish pulling up on a road beside the river. "We're here. This is the Lost Ravine Mining Co."

They pulled up next to a loading dock of a big supply store. Clint helped Irish unload the wagon. By the time they finished he understood why the man was so muscular.

"Hop on up," said Irish. "I'll pay you for your labor with a fine meal."

"Can't beat them wages," said Clint.

They drove back down the river road to the other side of the ravine and up a hill. The Lost Ravine Gold Mine was located between two monstrous hills with most of the town on one side and Irish's stables and tent town on the other. Irish drove the team in under a stable hall barn that was open on both ends. He stopped and got down.

Clint jumped down and untied Lady and led her to the back of the barn. He could hardly believe his eyes. They were looking out at about thirty acres of the greenest pasture he had ever seen, just like he had envisioned. "You can turn her out there if you like," said Irish, walking up beside Clint. And so he did.

They took care of the mules.

"Living quarters are around front," said Irish, leading the way.

After a fine meal Clint went around back to check on Lady. Irish followed him out. "Lad you'll break your back from sunup to sundown out in them gold fields," he said. "And all you'll get are a few nuggets and maybe a little dust. Just enough to buy supplies and go back and try again."

"Maybe so," said Clint. "You're the second man to tell me that. It sure is peaceful out here."

"Few men strike it big like them men over there," Irish said, pointing over the ravine at the big houses sitting on the side of the hills. "Everyone else is just picking up the droppings. You can make more money hauling supplies for all these people than you can digging for gold," he said, walking out to a half wagon sitting on blocks. "How about it Clint, throw in with me."

"I don't know," said Clint. "I never thought about driving a supply wagon before."

"Believe it or not," said Irish, "when this wagon is finished it will look just like the other one. I've got two extra mules already. They're grazing out there with Lady right now. Four more and we'd have another team. That'll double our pay load."

"Lady would have her green pasture that I promised her," said Clint.

"If we work really hard, we'll have that other wagon on the road in six months time," said Irish. "If you stay with me until it's finished, I'll make you a full partner."

"Let me sleep on it," said Clint.

Clint was up early the next morning working on the wagon when Irish came out, "Morning partner," said Irish.

"Morning," Clint answered.

CHAPTER 11

Six months later they had the wagon and team on the road.

Four years later they had eight teams and wagons going in all four directions, making two trips a week. Their hard work had paid off.

They passed the long nights and some days talking about the past.

Irish had come to this country as a small child with his parents. They were moving west with a wagon train when they caught the fever and died somewhere out on the trail. Irish was taken in by an old muler who taught him to read and write. He learned to drive a six-mule team by the time he was twelve years old. When the old man died Irish moved further and further west, hauling freight as he came. It was risky back then but the pay was good.

Clint told about growing up an orphan after his father was killed on a cattle drive, about going to work on a cattle ranch at twelve years of age and about going on his first round up and trail drive by the time he was sixteen. He told about his years on the trail and how after ten years he was almost broke so he turned west to find a better way of life. Mostly he talked about those that he had left in a little town called Bitter Creek. A beautiful woman named Sarah, with sad blue eyes, a little girl also named Sarah and of Old Az. He talked about how someday he was going back and get them.

He even wrote letters, ten or twelve of them, that never got mailed. "Someday, maybe," he would say.

Over the years Clint and Irish became very good friends.

Clint had been on a long haul and had broken down not far from town. Irish had come to find him. It was late by the time they made repairs and drove into the barn. They both noticed that Lady wasn't waiting by the gate at her usual place. Clint looked worried when he didn't see her.

"Go on and find her," said Irish. "I'll take care of the mules."

Clint walked out into the pasture. He didn't see her anywhere so he walked across the field to her favorite clover patch. There she lay and there he buried her.

Irish and all the drivers came to help. She had become a favorite and a pet to them all. She had a long and good life. They buried her deep and piled rocks on her grave to mark the place. Clint later fenced it off.

A few months later Clint drove in from a haul to Pineville. "Right on time," said Irish.

"Yep," said Clint. "The train tracks are almost here."

"How long?" asked Irish.

"Soon," said Clint. "Fast as they're laying that track, one maybe, two months."

"Think it will hurt our business any?" asked Irish.

"Maybe," said Clint, "not much though. I wonder how they are going to turn that train around so it can go back?" They got a good laugh out of that.

A month later the engine steamed into town, whistle blowing, bell ringing, scaring the mules and anything else with ears, out of their minds. Everyone was there to see it arrive. They had been waiting a long time for it to reach them.

"Well there goes the peace and quiet," said Clint.

"Yep, reckon so," said Irish.

A week later, the gold mine gave out. It just quit. They searched and dug and picked all over and found nothing. Panic set in and people started to leave, a few at first then a lot more followed.

Within a month tent town was completely deserted along with half the town. More were packing to leave every day. Clint and Irish were sitting in their office talking over their next move. They had nothing much to haul anymore so they were batting around ideas about what to do now. Neither wanted to leave. They really liked it here.

"Let's buy the mine," said Irish.

"With what?" asked Clint.

"With our savings," said Irish. "We can also sell the teams and wagons. We will buy the mine and as much of the land that goes with it as we can."

"What for?" asked Clint. "You said yourself that there is no money in digging for gold."

"Not for the gold," said Irish. "The timber. That sawmill just sits idle most of the time and they own the land on both sides of both forks of the river. Now that the railroad is here we have an easy way to haul it out."

Clint thought for a minute. "Let's do it," he said. "We'll keep one wagon. I'll offer the other seven to the men that drove them."

"Six hundred for each team and four hundred for each wagon," said Clint.

"Sounds fair to me," said Irish. "We'll talk to the men this evening. If they agree you can go to town tomorrow and settle the deal. I'll talk to the mine owners."

"Agreed," said Clint. "I think most of them will go for it. They are all good men."

"There is a lesson to be learned in that," said Irish.

"What do you mean?" asked Clint.

"I mean," said Irish, "they are all good men because we chose good men and they have stayed with us all these years because we paid a fair wage for a fair days work."

What he said next stuck with Clint for the rest of his life. "Son," said old Irish, "what goes around usually has a way of getting back to you sooner or later."

"That is one lesson I'll always remember," said Clint.

That evening the men all jumped at the chance to buy the wagons and teams. It was quite a ride back to the Lost Ravine. Clint was having second thoughts. Maybe he and Irish should take their money and leave like everyone else.

Clint was deep in thought when he turned the team into the barn and stopped. "Bam," the big door slammed as Irish ran outside interrupting the quiet. "Yahoo," he yelled, startling the mules. Clint almost jumped out of his seat.

"We bought the whole mountain. Yahoo," said Irish. "Five thousand acres, gold mine, sawmill and all for ten thousand dollars."

"All of it?" asked Clint. "That will take every dollar that we have."

"Yep, and worth every penny," said Irish. "Come on, they are waiting for us at the train. They can't wait to get out of here."

When they finished their business Clint and Irish watched the train huff, blow, and scrape. It slowly picked up speed and backed out of the valley taking the last of the people and their life's savings with it.

"Guess it don't have to turn around," said Irish.

"Reckon not," said Clint.

They continued to watch as the train rounded the bend and fade out of sight. It got quiet, real quiet. They could hear birds chirping. They could even hear the water rushing by in the river. What had been a busy little town was now all gone. They were the only two left.

"Sure is quiet," said Clint.

"Yep," said Irish. "We have got plenty of quiet all right, but what we need is cash if we are going to make this place work."

"We will start digging first thing in the morning," said Clint. "Let's see if there is any gold left in that hole."

The next morning they were getting ready to go to the mine when the train huffed back into the town. Old Coop, the engineer, walked up the hill to where Clint and Irish stood watching. "What do you want me to do with the train, boss, uh, bosses?" he asked.

Clint and Irish looked at each other. They were surprised. "I reckon we bought ourselves a train too," chuckled Clint.

"Guess so," said Irish.

"It's yours all right," said Coop. "It sure don't belong to anyone else."

"Well just turn it off or put it out or whatever you do," said Clint.

"Yes sir," said Coop. "Reckon I'm stuck here until you go to town."

"Can you cook, Coop?" asked Irish.

"Yep, some," said Coop.

"Then you'll cook. We'll dig, and you'll cook," said Clint. "At least until we get that sawmill up and running."

They picked and dug around that mine all winter until early spring. They had a few bags of gold dust and some nuggets to show for their work but did not have any big finds.

"Rainy season is coming," said Irish. "Better hitch up the wagon tomorrow and go to town before the road washes out."

"Reckon so," said Clint. "We'll cash in our find. Maybe we will have enough for a new start."

The next day they headed out early turning south on river road headed for the town of River Wells. The sky was already getting dark with clouds.

They arrived in River Wells to find it full of men out of work and down on there luck. Everyone was becoming desperate. As he drove toward, the bank Clint saw two men standing in front that made him very uneasy. They drove on past the bank. They turned and went around the corner into the alley and stopped behind the bank. Clint walked around front, went inside and told the banker he had gold to cash in and of the men out front. The banker knew Clint and Irish well. He quickly went and unlocked the back door to let them in. After conducting their business they left the same way.

Driving to the supply store, Clint noticed the two men following and alerted Irish and Coop. They decided it would be best if they didn't stay in town any longer than necessary. They finished up the other business they had and started home. The two men followed as they drove out of town. "Check your rifles," said Clint. "Keep them ready, we may have a fight on our hands."

About a half mile further they saw six more riders off in the trees. The two men rode off the road to meet them. Clint hurried the mules on. When they were about half-way home it started to rain. They could see dark clouds and lots of lightning over their mountain and knew they were in for a hard ride. The road was beginning to wash badly.

When they topped the next hill, they could see that the riders had given up and turned back toward town. "Keep an eye out for slides. We may have to leave the wagon and ride the mules," said Irish.

"Never rode a mule," said Coop.

"May be a good time to learn," said Clint.

The mules were pulling hard when they turned into the barn. They were just in time, the clouds opened up and poured. It poured rain on and off for most all the next month. The roads turned into mud filled with rushing dirty water and tree limbs.

Chapter 12

One morning they woke to a loud crashing and rumbling sound. The ground was shaking as they ran outside to see what was going on. They stood and watched across the ravine at the mountain on the other side as it turned to mud and began to slide down into the ravine. The mud began to fill the gold mine. As the mud slid down the side of the mountain, it brought with it, rocks, boulders and trees.

The two big fancy houses and half the town lay in the ravine before it stopped and the gold mine lay beneath thirty feet of mud and rubble. They stood and shook their heads as they stared at the mess before them.

"Well we still have our side of the mountain, for now anyway," said Clint.

"And the sawmill," said Irish. "That's a starting place."

"And the train," added Coop. "Let's have some breakfast."

It stopped raining a few days later and the sun came out shining. Clint walked outside and looked across the ravine at the other mountain. A place about a hundred feet almost straight up from the bottom of the ravine was shining like a new penny. "You better get out here, Irish," yelled Clint.

"What do you think that is?" asked Clint, pointing at the shiny spot.

"Don't know," said Irish. "But I aim to find out as soon as that mud dries a little."

It was two weeks before the mud dried enough to get up the mountain, but when they made it up, they found a vein of gold going back in the side of that hill the size of a wagon. All their dreams had come true.

"We're rich," said Irish. "Yahoo, we're rich."

"We are that," said Clint, picking up a big chunk of gold.

Clint carried the gold back down the hill. "Coop," he said, showing him the gold, "take one of the mules and go see what we'll need to repair that trestle. We're fixing to need that train back in operation. Decide what supplies and tools you'll need and how many men you need to get that train rolling."

"Yes sir boss," replied Coop. "Right away."

"We need to get on back up there," said Irish. "We need to hide that vein … before someone sees it and starts a gold rush all over again."

"Yep," said Clint. "We can hide it with mud and dry brush until we can get a walkway up to it."

"I'll break this chunk up into small pieces tonight before cashing it in," said Clint. "Maybe we won't draw much attention in town."

They climbed back up the mountain and smeared mud over the gold to cut down on the shine. They threw limbs and brush around to look as though the wind had dumped it there. They went back down and studied their handiwork. They decided they would need to work on it some more tomorrow.

The next morning Clint and Irish rode around the mountain and wound their way up to the top. They cut enough small trees to cover a wide area and dropped them over the side to the ledge below to finish hiding the gold.

The next two or three days they worked moving rocks and dirt. When they finished they had made a three foot wide walkway up the side of the mountain. Now they could easily get up to the vein of gold.

They hitched up the wagon early the next morning for a trip to town. They needed supplies and would also need to go by the bank and cash in enough gold to pay for them.

"That's pure gold," said the banker. "Did you fellers find another vein out there?" he asked jokingly.

"Nope," said Irish. "But there is a little more where that came from," he added, trying to hide their secret.

Clint noticed the same two shabby looking men hanging around out front that he had seen before. He warned Irish and Coop they were there. They loaded up the supplies, and now at last they were on the road heading for home. Clint hurried the mules along.

"Keep a close watch behind Coop," he said, rubbing the back of his neck.

That old feeling had returned, warning him they were being followed. He had learned to trust this feeling and it stayed with him all the way. They didn't have any problems and they all breathed a sigh of relief when they pulled up at the lost ravine.

The next morning Clint and Irish headed back up the mountain leaving Coop to his chores and making his list of needs. They had just reached the top when they heard gun fire back at the stable. Clint took cover behind a large rock on one side of the ledge and Irish ducked to the other side just as a spray of bullets ricocheted all around them.

Some men had run from the cabin and taken cover at the foot of the mountain. They had Clint and Irish boxed in. They could see no way out.

"Too late," said Irish. "They've seen us."

"Yep," said Clint. "They've probably been watching us all morning."

"How many do you see?" asked Irish.

"Six, seven, maybe eight," answered Clint.

"You think they got old Coop?" asked Clint.

"Most likely they did," answered Irish.

"Throw down the gold," came a voice echoing up from the bottom of the mountain. "We know it ain't in the cabin."

"We cashed it all in yesterday," yelled Clint. "You saw us." He knew it was the same men that he had seen hanging around the bank and that had followed them before.

"Then throw down the cash," came a second voice.

"We used it all for supplies," answered Irish.

"There are eight of us down here," came the first voice. "We've got you pinned down up there and we're prepared to wait you out … or starve you out. Just throw down the money and we'll leave you in peace."

"Looks like a long night," said Clint. "I'll take first watch."

They had a day's supply of food and water but after that it would be a waiting game. They took turns all night watching and sleeping.

The next morning the sun peeked over the top of the mountains behind them. It was quiet, too quiet to suit Clint, then suddenly three ear popping *boom, boom, boom's* shattered the quiet.

The men below scattered like ants. Two went flying through the air landing in the rubble of the ravine. Two more ran for the horses where they had hidden them behind a boulder. The man they had left to guard them lay on the ground and the horses were nowhere to be found.

"The horses are gone," said one.

"Tag's dead." yelled the other, just as Clint and Irish fired their rifles, knocking them to the ground.

Clint turned to see three more small streaks of smoke go by followed by three more loud *boom, boom, boom's*. The last three men ran from their hiding place with their hands in the air begging not to be shot. "We give up, we give up, don't shoot," they shouted.

"Come out in the clear," yelled Clint. "Throw them rifles in the ravine."

The men did as they were told still not sure they were not going to be shot.

"Drop them side guns and knives down on the ground," yelled Irish.

"Now climb up on that flat rock and sit down facing yonder way," said Clint. He heard someone calling out to him, "I'm coming down, don't shoot me."

"That you up there Coop," yelled Clint.

"Yes, it's me all right," came a reply.

"Thought it might be," said Clint, glad to hear his voice. "We were afraid they got you."

"Nope, they didn't," said Coop.

"Well come on down then," said Clint. "Keep these guys covered, Irish."

Clint walked down the path and stood behind the men. Without saying a word he waited for Irish and Coop.

When Coop arrived he was riding one of the outlaw's horses and leading the other seven.

Clint turned to the outlaws and ordered them to come down where he was. "Pick up your two friends, or what's left of them and throw them across those saddles. We'll give them a proper burial."

Irish went over to the men that were wounded. "One is shot bad in the shoulder," he said. "The other one was hit in the leg."

"Well let's get them up to the house," said Clint. "We'll take then to town tomorrow and turn them over to the sheriff."

The three outlaws sighed with relief. The two wounded men grumbled, "We can't walk up that hill."

"You can," yelled Clint, "or I'll leave you out here for buzzard bait."

After burying the three outlaws they tied the other outlaws up. Old Coop explained that he had slipped through the escape hatch when he saw the outlaws ride up. When they shot the lock off the lock box he hid behind the false wall until dark then crawled out and went to the storage shed. He took up the floor, got a satchel full of dynamite, and the rest you know he explained.

"Well you sure earned your place here today," said Clint.

"Sure did," said Irish. "As long as you want."

"You would've done the same for me," said Coop.

"I would," said Clint. "Just the same if you ever have a need, just say."

"I like things just the way they are," said Coop. "What do you want me to do with these horses anyway?"

"Turn them out to pasture," said Clint. "They ain't gonna need them where they're going."

"Yes," said Irish "They should be going away for a long time. They owe us at least as much as those horses are worth for all the trouble they caused."

The outlaws began to look worried again. It would be a long time before they learned that they had been looking straight at one of the richest gold finds in history and didn't even know it.

CHAPTER 13

A year later the gold mine, as well as the sawmill, was running at full speed. People began to return. Homes were being built. Businesses were opening. Clint was rebuilding the town close to the bottom of the hill. He made a big open square in the middle overlooking the rail station and river. He planted grass, flowers and trees. The town was booming. Everything looked fresh and clean.

Clint's office was at the highest point, right in the center of the square, with a big window in front so he could watch all the operations at the same time. He had a sign hung over his door: *The James Mill and Mining Co.* That's the way old Irish wanted it. The name stuck and so the town of James Mill came into being.

Irish was busy these days. When he wasn't fishing or cooking the fish that he caught, he was drawing diagrams of his dream house. He had retired and picked a nice spot up stream. The house would overlook the river in front and the town on the side. He would have windows all around the front and side.

One day Irish walked into Clint's office. "We'd better hire a marshal," he said. "The town is growing. Our train is coming in full every week. We need to keep order."

"Agreed," said Clint. "I'll take care of it today."

Clint knew that wasn't what was bothering Irish so he waited for more.

"What's wrong?" asked Clint.

"I'm getting old," said Irish.

"I've noticed," chuckled Clint. "What else?"

"Well," said Irish, "I'm rich beyond my wildest dreams. More money than I can ever spend. I'd like to go see part of this world. Maybe go to Ireland and see the place where I was born."

"I think that's a good idea," said Clint. "I can run things here. I'll build your dream house for you while your gone. "Just like you drew it."

"I may not come back," said Irish. "I have a lot I want to see. I don't have any family you know. Except you, you're like a son to me."

"I know," said Clint.

"Well, I want you to have this place. All of it," said Irish. "I'll sign the papers before I go."

"When are you leaving?" asked Clint.

"Next week," said Irish. "I've made up my mind."

And he did. It was a hard parting for Clint, he had grown very fond of the old man, but they said their good byes.

It was several months later that the marshal walked into Clint's office, "Old Coop's got a special shipment for you over at the train station," he said.

"What is it?" asked Clint.

"Don't know," said the marshal, "but it is something from Irish."

Clint hurried across the town square to the train station, "What is it Coop?" he asked.

"You got to see it for your self," said Coop, walking to a box car and sliding back the big door.

Clint pushed his hat to the back of his head and with his hands on his side, he just stared. There standing in the middle of the boxcar was a life size statue of a salt and pepper gray. The horse was standing in a field of green with the name LADY across the bottom in big block letters.

"It came all the way from Paris, France," said Coop. "What do you want me to do with her boss?"

"That old man just might spend all that money after all," said Clint, more or less to himself.

"Get me some masons, Coop," said Clint. "Have them build a stand six feet high dead center of town square. Set her right on top."

"Yes sir," said Coop.

The town continued to grow and prosper. Clint was still working on the dream house. It took about six months but Clint had finally put the finishing touches on Irish's dream house. He had decided to call it *The Irishman's Dream*. When he got back to his office, the marshal came in. "A man over at the train station is asking for you," he said. "He said his name is Azera or something like that."

"Azaria Cain," said Clint, jumping up so fast he sent his chair sliding across the floor.

He hurried around his desk and across the town square at almost a run and into the station house. Clint scanned the room full of people until he found Az across the room and hurried over to shake his hand.

"Glad you finally made it," said Clint. "What took you so long anyway?"

"Might never have made it," said Az, "if it hadn't been for an old Irishman that came by a few months back. He told us where you were and how you struck it rich. He gave us free passes on the train all the way out here and all the money you sent."

"Money? I never …! That's old Irish for you," said Clint, shaking his head. "You couldn't have come at a better time," he added. "I sure could use some help running this place. You said US?"

"Got a surprise for you," said Az, moving to one side.

There sitting on a bench behind him was little Sarah, looking all grown up.

Clint just stood and stared. "I can't believe it," he said. "You're all grown up."

"I sure am," she said, wrapping both arms around his neck so tight he thought his head would pop off.

Clint was looking all around the room searching every face.

"She's in the powder room," said Az and Sarah at almost the same time.

"I'll go get her," said Sarah.

"Was I that obvious?" asked Clint.

"You were to someone that's been there," said Az, with a laugh.

"She was shaking like a leaf in a whirlwind when we got here," said Az, "not knowing what to expect."

"It's been almost seven years, Clint. She gave up on ever seeing or hearing from you again a long time ago. If it hadn't been for them letters you wrote, she may not of come."

Clint was afraid she hadn't come and now he was afraid because she had.

Little Sarah rounded the corner with his Sarah in hand and stopped.

Clint just stared for a long minute and then his two left feet got tangled as he tried to hurry over.

"I was afraid you didn't come," he said. "I mean I'm glad you came. I don't know what I mean."

"All that matters is that we are here now," said Sarah.

"That's what I wanted to say," said Clint. "Let's get you all moved up to the house. You must be worn out. It's real comfortable up there. Quiet too."

"Coop get a luggage wagon," yelled Clint. "Bring it around front. You drive it."

"Yes sir, boss," said Coop, hoping he would get to meet the new folks.

Clint helped them move their luggage to the loading dock and then into the wagon when Coop drove around.

When they all got into the wagon Old Coop was just beaming.

"OK Coop," said Clint. "Folks this is Fanagan Cooper, he drives the train and just about anything else that moves."

"This one's Az, Azaria Cain," said Clint. "And this is Sarah and Sarah, soon to be James, I hope," his face turning red. "Now get us up to the house," he ordered jokingly.

"Yes sir, boss," said Coop, with a big grin.

They drove through the gate to the big house and little Sarah read the sign over it: "*The Irishman's Dream,"* she read. "Why do you call it that?" she asked.

"It belongs to my partner," said Clint. "It's his dream house, if he ever comes back. I had it built for him," added Clint.

"He must be a real friend," said Sarah.

"He's a lot more than that," said Clint. "You met him. He's the old Irishman that came to Bitter Creek to get you."

Clint got them all moved in the big house. The two Sarahs fell in love with it right away, going from room to room, upstairs and down, making plans to decorate.

Az explained to Clint how Bitter Creek had gone belly up. Sutterfield had invested everything he had into the town and lost it all. When the trails moved north and bypassed the town, everyone left and it just dried up.

Later that night after everyone else had gone to bed, Sarah came downstairs where Clint was sitting and looking out across his town.

"What are you thinking about?" she asked.

"I'm thinking about selling all the store buildings. I would like to sell them to each of the shopkeepers that runs them," said Clint. "A town should be owned and governed by the people that live in it."

"I couldn't agree more," said Sarah. "I've seen what can happen to a town where everything is owned by one man."

"Then I'll get started first thing in the morning," said Clint.

Sarah took the letters out of her pocket that Clint had written over the years. "Irish gave them to me," she said, "and I read them. That's what convinced me to come here. Why didn't you mail them Clint? We thought you had forgotten about us."

"I didn't" said Clint. "I thought about you a lot when I was by myself. I just didn't have anything to offer you and didn't know if I ever would."

"Do you think that would have mattered?" asked Sarah.

"I don't know," said Clint. "I almost asked you to come with me that night at the diner back in Bitter Creek … it seems like so long ago now. After I got here I was so busy trying to make a go of it, the days and months turned into years. They passed so fast … by the time I did strike it rich I thought it was too late."

"I thought about you a lot after you left," said Sarah. "For some reason you gave me back the hope that I had lost. But as time passed the memories faded and along with them the hope did too."

They did not talk much about the past after that night. They concentrated on the future and their life together.

"Did you mean what you said a while ago? About me … being Mrs. James, I mean."

"I did," said Clint. "If you'll have me, I would like to marry you."

"I will," said Sarah. "I will be happy to marry you."

Just then little Sarah danced into the room hopping up and down. She was sobbing tears of joy and trying to talk at the same time. "This has been my wish all these years. I just knew you hadn't forgotten about us, I just knew you didn't." She had been sitting on the stairs, with both fingers crossed, listening.

"Clint, I know that you are a good man and an honest man. I feel like I know you," said Sarah. "But I would like to have some time to really get to know you before we are married."

"That's OK," said Clint, "take as much time as you need. You need to be sure."

"Oh, I am sure," said Sarah. "I would marry you today if that's what you want. However, I would like to make some plans. I need time to let all this soak in."

"You and little Sarah will stay here," Clint said. "I have a small house behind my office. It's left over from the old town and it's close to my work."

They all sat, talked and made plans until the early morning sun began lighting the day.

Chapter 14

About two weeks later a young man walked into Clint's office leading a black and white shaggy dog.

"Mr. James?" he asked. "Clinton James?"

"Yep," said Clint. "Lucky, is that you boy?"

Lucky immediately came to Clint.

"You know the dog then?" asked the young man.

"Yep," said Clint. "We go back aways."

"My name is Elbert Weatherspoon the III," he said, handing Clint a sealed letter. "From Orchard," he added. "I'm here on behalf of my grandfather to deliver this letter and the dog."

Clint opened the letter. It read: *Clint, if you are reading this letter, the young man standing in front of you is my grandson. He just graduated from law school. Thought you might point him in the right direction. Keep an eye on him and Lucky for me. I'm getting too old to chase after them anymore. He's a good kid. Elb.*

After reading the letter Clint looked up and asked, "How would you like to come to work for me Elb?"

"I'd like it," he said.

"Then we'll get you settled in," said Clint. "I need a lawyer. I want to make a lot of changes around here. First I want to open a bank."

A month later old Irish came in on the train and moved back into his old stable house. He said the old house was the thing he missed most while he was gone. That's what he wanted and that's what he got.

Irish and Az became good friends and fishing buddies.

After six months proper courting Clint and Sarah were married right out in the middle of town square next to Lady's statue. "It's a fitting place for the town's founder to get married," someone was heard to say. "And the only place big enough for the whole town to gather," said another. A while later they adopted little Sarah so she would have a real last name.

Elb stayed busy getting the town set up like Clint wanted. The bank had been started and most of the stores were now owned by people in the town. Clint began to notice that since he had hired the young lawyer, little Sarah found more and more reasons to stop by his office. He was getting suspicious that more was going on than met the eye. All those after supper walks, hand-in-hand and the Sunday picnics. "Little Sarah and Elb," he thought. He decided he liked the idea.

It was early spring, one of those crisp mornings with a gentle warm breeze. Clint propped open the front door to his office and sat down in the big chair behind his desk. He pushed it back so he could lean on the wall, propped his boots up on his desk and pulled his hat down over his eyes. Not to sleep, but to think.

Clint knew that little Sarah sometimes thought about her real family. Even though she hardly ever talked about it, she knew that her family was buried somewhere out on the frontier. She often wondered if she had any other relatives.

Clint had decided to see if he could find any information on her family. About six months back he had hired the Browning Detective Agency in St. Louis. He asked them to track down as much information as they could about the wagon train the two Sarahs had come west with. He talked with big Sarah and they sent Browning everything they knew, which wasn't much. She had remembered the date the wagon train left St. Louis and the names of some of the people. The only thing little Sarah ever remembered was a small painted chest with a picture of a bird on it. She was so young when it happened that she had forgotten everything a long time ago. She had a faint memory of her father being tall and kind.

Browning himself took on the case, sending progress letters ever month or two. He had little to report until two months ago. Clint received a letter from Browning. He could almost read the excitement in the man's handwriting.

Browning had found an old wagon scout that had been with the wagon train. The old scout told of how news of the tragedy had spread far and wide. The trail used by that train had never been used again. Browning and the scout were on their way to try and find that trail.

Two weeks ago Clint received a second letter from Browning. He told about finding the abandoned wagons strewn along the trail. Some of the wagons were burned, but most were not. What remained told the story of tragedy that had fallen upon that wagon train. They had come upon several wagons that had long since weathered out. One revealed a false bottom. Under the floor was a small trunk with a picture of a bird on it, maybe a Robin, nothing else was found.

The trunk was in bad condition but intact. It was carefully crated and Browning himself was to accompany it to James Mill. He would arrive on next Saturday's noon train. "It's time to tell little Sarah what I've been up to," thought Clint.

Elb came into his office for the second time and shuffled around nervously with some papers. "Not like Elb," thought Clint. The hair on back of his neck stiffened. That old feeling was warning him something was up.

The two Sarahs had used up the winter planning to build a new school as soon as the weather permitted. The town was growing. The kids needed a school. They reasoned that if Uncle Irish could draw plans for such a beautiful house he could draw plans for a new school. With Uncle Az's knowledge of wood and Uncle Coop's ability to find and haul just about anything, the school would soon be well on the way up.

A familiar voice from outside interrupted Clint's thoughts. It was little Sarah "whoaing" her horse and buggy to a halt in front of his office.

Clint pushed his hat back in its place on his head and let his boots drop hard to the floor. He stood up just as Elb hurried back into his office … for the third time.

Sarah was with little Sarah and neither had waited to be helped down. Now he was sure something was up and he was pretty sure of what it was.

The two Sarahs walked through the door with big smiles and stood next to Elb, who looked as white and wet from sweat as a just washed sheet.

"What's the occasion?" Clint asked., trying not to look suspicious. Just then Irish, Az and Coop sneaked in the door.

"Well," said Elb, "Oh … sir … sir … oh."

"Sir," replied Clint.

"Well, I mean, Mr."

"Mr.?," Clint asked.

"Clint," said Elb, as he straightened up and his color returned. "I would like to ask for your daughter's hand in marriage. We would like your blessing."

"When's the wedding?" Clint asked.

"As soon as our new home can be built," said Sarah.

"Where will you build it?" asked Clint.

"Just over the ridge from you and Sarah, facing the river," answered Elb.

"Good Pick," said Clint.

Elb took out the papers he had been shuffling around. "These are the drawings of our new home," he said. "Irish has been working on them along with the school."

"Oh," said Clint, looking at the three old men. "So you've been in on this all along, have you?"

"Well, yes, yeah, yep, we have," they all agreed, looking wishfully at the open door.

"Guess the whole town knows about it except ME," Clint said jokingly.

"No, nope, nah," they all agreed. "Not ever last one of them." added Coop. They all had a needed laugh.

Clint turned to stand in front of little Sarah. He put both hands on her shoulders and held her at arms length. He looked straight into her eyes and said, "You're not my little Sarah anymore are you? One day when I wasn't looking you grew into a beautiful woman." He took her hand and gave it to Elb. "You have my blessing. I am very pleased. Sarah James Weatherspoon, sure has a nice ring to it."

"Well, this is a day for surprises," Clint said, handing Sarah the last two letters he had gotten from Browning.

"You and Elb read these. We planned on sharing this with you today."

"I don't know what to say," little Sarah said after reading the letters. "That's just a few days from now."

"Don't say anything for now," Clint said. "Your mother wanted your waiting time to be as short as possible, in case this doesn't pan out."

Saturday was a long time in coming but at last they were all again gathered in Clint's office. Old Coop went alone to collect Mr. Browning and the trunk. The train was on time and the wait was short. Coop stopped his wagon outside Clint's office. The man sitting next to him was tall. He had wide shoulders that filled out his dark suit. He looked like a man that was never out of place, no matter where he was.

Mr. Browning easily carried the crate inside and set it on Clint's desk. He turned, "Adam Browning," he said. "But my friends call me Brownie."

Clint introduced everyone to Brownie. When he finished, Brownie turned and popped the top off the crate and lifted out the little trunk. "I believe this is for you, Miss," he said.

Sarah drew her breath, "That's it," she said in a muffled whisper from behind her hands. "That is the trunk I remember."

"We left the trunk intact and unopened," Brownie said. "We thought you should be the first to see what's inside."

Sarah stood staring down at the little trunk with both hands on the lid. She said, "No matter what we find inside, you all will always be my real family, I know that now."

Clint twisted the lock pulling it away from the rotted wood and Sarah opened the lid. Rats had long past gnawed their way in and left nothing recognizable but four gold coins. The coins were probably all that was left of the family's life savings. Some empty spools and rusty needles told that it was probably a woman's sewing box used to make and mend her family's clothes.

Sarah looked more relieved than anything else. "And now it's finished," she said. "I would like to place this trunk in a place of honor in our new home. I think up high just below the balcony floor and in full view of the front entrance."

"When we come through the door and see it," she said. "It will remind us all that we have families somewhere out on the prairie."

Chapter 15

Clint smiled when he looked up and saw Elb and Sarah's buggy come from behind the tree line. They turned on the road coming down a long easy hill toward their new house. They came almost every day at lunch to check on the progress. An early fall wedding had been planned. Everything had to be finished.

"Howdy," Clint said, as they drew up in front of the house.

"Howdy," they both replied, as Sarah jumped off the buggy and ran inside.

"It was hard to tell who was the most excited," Clint thought. "Me and Sarah or Elb and Sarah or them three old men she so fondly calls uncles."

"Don't forget, we have a one o'clock meeting," Clint said as he mounted up. He wanted to make Sarah and Elb full partners in all his holdings as a wedding gift.

"I'll be there," Elb said.

Neither of them suspected that not far away, hiding in the trees, two old enemies were watching, plotting and planning to do them harm. They were cruel and heartless men willing to do anything for money.

Clint looked at his clock. "One fifteen," he thought. "It's not like Elb to be late."

Twenty minutes later Clint stood up to go out back for his horse. The back of his neck was tingling telling him something had gone wrong. He hadn't taken two steps before he heard a familiar voice ringing out loud and clear across the town square. A voice he had heard a thousand times before. "Hee-yaw, hee-yaw, pull, pull." It was Irish and he was coming hard and fast.

Clint ran out the door in time to see Irish go by driving Elb's team with one hand and hanging on to Elb with the other. "He's hurt bad," Irish yelled as he "*whoa'd*" in front of the doctor's clinic.

Clint hurried around to help Elb down. "Who done this?" he asked. "Where's Sarah," he almost yelled. Elb tried to mumble something that made no sense.

When they got Elb on the doc's table, Irish handed Clint a note. "This was in his top pocket." Clint unfolded the paper. *WE GOT THE GURL. IF YOU WANT HER BAK IN ONE PEAS BRING 10,000 DOLLARS TO THE BLUFF AND TOSS IT OVER. COME ALONE OR THE DEAL IS OFF.*

"Kidnaped," Clint said aloud just as Coop and Az came in.

"Who, Sarah?" they asked.

"Yep," said Irish.

"Irish get our horses," said Clint. "We've got some tracking to do. Coop, take the buckboard downstream to the tannery. Get Arkansas. Tell him to bring his bloodhounds. We're going to need them. Az, go get the marshal, then go up to the house and get Sarah. Bring her back here to help with Elb. You stay with them."

"Yes sir boss," Coop and Az echoed.

When Clint went outside Irish was coming around the corner with the horses. "Take me to where you found Elb," Clint said as he mounted up. "Let's ride."

Clint and Irish scouted around the field until they found the outlaw's tracks. "Looks like they're heading north, up river into the rocks," Clint said. Just then the marshal and about a dozen men rode up.

"Fan out," said the marshal. "We're going to need all the luck we've got to track them varmints."

About a quarter mile up they lost the trail and there was no finding it. "Our luck hasn't run out yet," Clint said, looking back down the trail. It was Coop with Arkansas and his bloodhounds.

"Hot dang," said the marshal. "I forgot about him."

"Thanks for coming, Arkansas," Clint said. "We sure need those dogs right now."

"Glad to help," said Arkansas. "Have you got anything of the girl's?" he asked. "The dogs need a scent."

"Anyone?" asked Clint.

Az came riding up the trail. He handed Clint a white bonnet. "Sarah said the dogs would need this. Elb's going to be just fine."

Clint looked relieved. "Thanks Az." He pitched the bonnet to Arkansas.

"When them dogs pick up the scent we'll have to hurry to keep up with them," said Arkansas. It wasn't a long wait. They followed the dogs uphill paralleling the river. They had been following the dogs for about twenty minutes when a spray of bullets sent them all ducking for cover. Their eyes searched the rocks to see where the shots came from.

The marshal tapped Clint on the shoulder and pointed straight ahead. There between the rocks and boulders, almost hidden by scrub brush, was an old trapper's cabin. It was so old it had faded right into the background. With the fall leaves still on you would have to know right where it was to find it. A man could walk right past and not see it.

The marshal signaled his men to surround the old cabin. Clint, the marshal and the rest crawled up the hill, staying behind the boulders until they were within thirty feet of the front door. "You men inside," Clint yelled. "You've got my daughter."

"We've got her. Did you bring the money?"

"We've got twenty men out here. You're surrounded. There is no way out," Clint yelled.

The outlaws answered with a wild shot hitting somewhere off to Clint's right. Clint tied Sarah's white bonnet to the end of his rifle barrel and waved it in the air. He stood up, his hands raised and walked to within fifteen feet of the front porch.

The door banged open and Sarah was pushed out in front of a big man half hidden behind the wall. "Say your piece," said the outlaw.

"Are you OK, Sarah?" Clint asked. She nodded yes. "I walked up here in the open like this so you will know I mean what I say. There is no real harm done up till now." Clint pleaded, "Give it up. Let her go and I'll promise you a fair trial. You may go to jail for a while but you'd still be alive."

"I ain't going back to jail," said the big outlaw.

"Then I promise you this," said Clint. "You harm one hair on her head and the inside of that cabin is the last thing you'll ever see."

Clint could hear the outlaws arguing. "I've had enough," one of them said. "I'm going out. You coming kid?"

A younger, taller man pushed past the bigger man who was still blocking the door. He tossed his pistol out in front of Clint and raised his hands. As the man walked toward Clint the big man shot him in the back, yelling, "Ain't no one walking out on me and living to tell about it." The man staggered toward Clint. "The … kid," he said, "innocent … nothing to do … with this." Then he dropped face down on the ground.

The big outlaw cocked his pistol as he raised it toward Clint. A shot was fired from inside the cabin hitting the outlaw in the back of his neck. He went limp then fell back against the door. Sarah broke free and ran to Clint. He pushed Sarah behind him where she was quickly surrounded by the three old men forming a human shield around her, protecting her from any further danger. The big man raised his pistol toward the other outlaw. Clint leveled his rifle and fired one shot. The big man fell to the floor. "You inside, come on out."

Shortly a young boy came to the door and raised his hands. "No more than sixteen," thought Clint. The boy walked to the man on the ground and knelt to one knee putting his hand on the man's shoulder. "Is he kin?" asked Clint. "My brother," said the boy. "My only kin."

"He said you're innocent that you had nothing to do with this."

"He is innocent," Sarah said, pushing her way to the front. "He tried to get them to let me go. He even offered to bring me home safely, but they wouldn't let him."

"What's your name boy?" asked Clint.

"Davey Hart," he answered. "My brother's name is Billy. The other man went by Scars because he had a bad leg. They just got out of prison. All they talked about was coming back here and getting even with the three old miners that sent them up."

"Two of the men that tried to rob us back in the old days," said Irish.

"Yep," said Clint. "Come on Davey, we'll help you bury your kin and then see if we can get you set on the right road. I owe you that much, you likely saved my life."

When they returned to town, the men were all tired and hungry. Elb had a headache but he was up and around.

Fall was in its full festival of colors when the wedding day arrived. Sarah and Elb were married standing on the front porch of their new home, surrounded by their family and friends that now included two old bloodhounds. The whole town had turned out.

Epilogue

A few months later the marshal was riding across the town square with three vagrants, cuffed and tied, walking in front of his horse. Old Coop had spotted them jumping the train back in Pineville.

The tall man stopped, "Wait, wait marshal," he said. "I know that horse there and the man that rode her. His name wouldn't be Clint James would it."

"It would," said the marshal. "But that's Mr. James to you."

"I gave him a hand a while back when he was down on his luck," said the man. "He might do the same for me."

"He does have a soft spot for a man that's down on his luck, said the marshal. "He'll give you a job if you ask for one and are willing to work."

"He may not even remember me," said the man, looking almost hopeful that he wouldn't.

"Well you're about to get a chance to ask him," said the marshal. "Here he comes now."

"Howdy marshal," said Clint. "Three more I see."

"Yep," said the marshal. "That one there says he knows you. Said he gave you a hand one time."

"You remember me don't you, Mr. James. Sutterfield, from Bitter Creek."

"Yep, I remember all right," said Clint. "Place left a bad taste in my mouth. But you did give me a hand up when I needed it," Clint said. "And I'll do the same for you if you want it. Pays a dollar a day and all you can eat at the diner," Clint said. "Take it or leave it. Goes for you other men, too."

"I'll take it," said Sutterfield.

"You'll be working for old Az. You remember him don't you?"

Sutterfield nodded.

"He runs the mill for me. I'll tell him to expect you in the morning. You can camp downstream a ways at the old tent town site," Clint said. "There's fish and small game there. You'll make out all right until you're back on your feet."

"Reckon the old Irishman was right after all," said Clint.

"How's that?" asked Sutterfield.

"What goes around," Clint said as he turned to go back to his office. "What goes around."

THE END

WILD FLOWERS

While traveling across our great country,
With all its wonders and beauty to behold,
None stays in my memory,
Like the wild flowers that grows along the road.

In a rainbow of color,
They populate the meadows, valleys and the hills,
So eager to spread their beauty,
The little dandelions, goldenrods, and daffodils.

You don't have to go far to see them,
Though they mostly are unnoticed,
So their beauty goes untold,
The little wild flowers that grows along the road.

Tom D. Bryant

LOOK FOR

What Goes Around: A Western Adventure

and

The Tree House Adventures: A Treasure Chest of Time

by

Tom D. Bryant

AT

www.iuniverse.com

Can Be Ordered
at
Most Major Book Stores
OR
Call 1-800-AUTHORS

978-0-595-45664-2
0-595-45664-2

Printed in the United States
88770LV00006B/277-300/A

9 780595 456642